Flicking idly through the pages of this sumptuous volume, and feeling a little depressed – even shaken – by the shocking revelatio character, you may well be wondering of the authors.

In fact, amidst a host o that they gleaned from astral investigators Vin vertible evidence to sugg people on Earth not born under any Sign.

SAYERS AND VINEY

The Bad News Zodiac

GRAFTON BOOKS
A Division of the Collins Publishing Group

LONDON GLASGOW
TORONTO SYDNEY AUCKLAND

Grafton Books
A Division of the Collins Publishing Group
8 Grafton Street, London W1X 3LA

Published by Grafton Books 1985

ISBN 0-586-06693-4

Printed and bound in Great Britain by
Collins, Glasgow

Set in Palatino

For
Becky & Tom
with thanks to
Madeleine

INTRODUCTION

Everyone reads the Stars, knows their Sign of the Zodiac and what their astrological characteristics are supposed to be. Everyone is only too happy to believe what Linda Goodman, Russell Grant and Co. tell them, i.e. you're a fabulously successful person, charismatic, creative and – wait for it – fatally attractive.

But not everyone can be successful, charismatic, creative and attractive. Like it or not hardly anyone really fits the bill. The stark reality is that there are an awful lot of extremely boring, extremely unsuccessful and fatally *un*attractive people out there. And as for charismatic – for all they know it's a type of camera.

Think of those people – the ones you work with, the ones you work for, your relatives, your friends, and – dare we whisper it – *yourself* – all with Star Signs, all with severe character defects. Something somewhere has gone wrong with Astrology. In your heart of hearts you always knew it was too good to be true, but can you face the real truth about yourself and everyone else? Can you face *The Bad News Zodiac*?

	Zodiac Sign and House		Ruling Planet	Element
	1st Aries	March 21–April 20	Mars	Fire
	2nd Taurus	April 21–May 21	Venus	Earth
	3rd Gemini	May 22–June 21	Mercury	Air
	4th Cancer	June 22–July 23	Moon	Water
	5th Leo	July 24–August 23	Sun	Fire
	6th Virgo	August 24–September 23	Mercury	Earth
	7th Libra	September 24–October 23	Venus	Air
	8th Scorpio	October 24–November 22	Mars/Pluto	Water
	9th Sagittarius	November 23–December 21	Jupiter	Fire
	10th Capricorn	December 22–January 20	Saturn	Earth
	11th Aquarius	January 21–February 19	Saturn/Uranus	Air
	12th Pisces	February 20–March 20	Jupiter/Neptune	Water

Fixed Aspect	Zodiac Character	Intergalactic Position at Birth	Long-term Astral Predictions	Planetary Colour
Wind	Childish	Mars throws a tantrum	Still not toilet trained	Teddy Bear yellow
Gas	Conformist	8.20 arrives on time	Still unpopular	Pinstripe
Malibu	Criminal	Mercury breaks into Milky Way	20 years	Behind bars blue
Pepsi	Wet	Watery Moon	Replaced by computer	Digital green
L.A.	Flash	Sun/Moon boogey!	Gross indecency	Spandex gold
Perrier	Hypo	Pluto deodorises	Change of hairstyle?	N.H.S. White
Dandruff	Indecisive	Venus all over the shop	Dandruff still there	Can't decide
Paraquat	Sadistic	Planets arm wrestling	Molestation charge	Blood red
Nitro-glycerine	Clumsy	Raging inferno	Asbestos suit	Burnt Sienna
Triumph TR7	Unscrupulous	Saturn rips off Jupiter	Digital cufflinks	Shark grey
Solar energy	Freaky	Saturn/Uranus on bad vibes trip	Will not part with Easy Rider album	Bean green
Nothing	Pathetic	Who cares?	None.	Invisible

ARIES

ARIES

March 21st–April 20th

'Who stole my porridge?'

Goldilocks and THE THREE BEARS

Aries is the sign of the Ram – strong, even a little stubborn – single-minded, dynamic, charismatic, fearless and confident. Idealistic, maybe, but headed for the top as well.

If you know an Aries man or woman, you will know that this description is entirely false, a criminal myth perpetuated through the ages by charlatan fortune-tellers more anxious to flatter than to tell the truth. Because the truth about Arietans is far from nice.

In fact, Mars holds a very strong Zodiacal position in the Aries chart and seems to frighten Aries children at birth in such a way that they never attain true adulthood. Aries people are indeed strong-willed, but in the most immature way imaginable. They can think only of themselves and the immediate gratification of their petty desires. And while children can be forgiven for being childish, it's harder to accept full-grown men and women behaving like infants. Arietans always want and never give. They throw tantrums and sulks; they cheat and steal with pathetic transparency and then deny it on oath. They eat sweets all day and like to say naughty words in front of old people. Spoilt in their youth (particularly by Pisces parents) they simply never grow up.

Most Arietans are equipped only to join the ranks of life's losers. Just occasionally, however, some evidence does surface to give credence to the myth of the Aries will to succeed. For, like the permanent children they are, Aries people have to be the centre of attention and hate to be ordered around by others. And sometimes, despite an almost total lack of ability, the stars will conspire to give them success. They will do well in any job that involves being driven around in a limo, being fêted in expensive restaurants, being surrounded by yes-men and doing no real work whatsoever . . . in short they make excellent film stars, TV personalities, and managing directors. These rare Arietans are always deeply deeply and deservedly hated, but the more numerous failures are not exactly well-liked either.

In short Aries people choose never to come to terms with the complexity and sophistication of the modern world. They prefer to leave that kind of hassle to *Thunderbirds*. More ordinary people have to try and sort their lives out for themselves. They can do without having to care for an Arietan.

THE ARIES MAN

The Aries man (quite clearly a contradiction in terms!) is very fond of his toys and it would be foolish to drag him away from his Lego set without being prepared for a tantrum. He likes games, but is such a terribly bad loser that few people will play with him twice. He doesn't have the patience to learn anything properly. Despite the fact that he may arrive at work on a microlite, the Aries man doesn't leave home until he is at least thirty, and then it is only to marry a woman as similar to his mother as possible. This unfortunate female will soon find herself supporting a family in which the father is the most troublesome child of all.

For in spite of his inbuilt affinity with kids, the Aries man makes an awful parent, being jealous, competitive and cruel. Only an Aries father could get up earlier than his children on Christmas morning in order to open their presents. Later that afternoon, Dad starts to eye up his three-year-old's new football and invites him out into the snowy garden to play. Immediately, he places the astonished mite in goal and proceeds to boot the ball past him for hour after freezing hour, pausing only to take the imagined applause of the Wembley crowd.

Aries men run to fat from an early age. They find it hard to walk past pâtisseries and pubs. They are fond of digital cufflinks. They demand constant praise for doing remarkably little. They make useless friends and hopeless lovers. They are despised by all and sundry.

THE ARIES WOMAN

The Aries woman is a sheep. In all things frivolous and fashionable, she follows the herd. In everything else, she follows her own entirely selfish whim.

Like her male counterpart, the Aries woman is happiest in childhood surroundings, and when she finally does leave the parental home, she will be taking with her a formidable collection of teddy bears, dolls and Paddington books.

As she grows older (she never grows *up*) she begins to get the taste for more toys – pearl necklaces, giant fridge-freezers, fur coats, country houses and convertible Mercedes, for example – and to look for the kind of sugar-daddy who can provide them. For as long as this romantic old imbecile is prepared to pay up, all will be well. When he decides he's got writer's cramp, just watch out for the frenzy of foot-stamping passion our little friend can muster. An Aries woman denied her own way is not a pretty sight.

Very occasionally, with Saturn sliding edgeways in the chart, the Aries woman will achieve a position of some consequence, but left to her own devices the Aries female is usually quite helpless. She may be found in a sordid mess of unwashed clothes and half-eaten chocolates, desperately searching the kitchen for a new bottle of pop.

As a parent, she is a disaster on the same scale as the male. The Aries mother starts by stealing her daughter's dolls, then later tries for her boyfriends. Spot her dancing voluptuously at the poor girl's sixteenth birthday party, then blowing out all the candles on the cake.

All in all, an Aries woman spells little but bad news.

ARIES SEX

Men

When an Aries man invites you back to his penthouse apartment for some 'fun and games' you can bet your life you may not have much fun, but you'll certainly get the games: the attic full of Meccano, Scalextric, jigsaws and Star Wars suits. Many are the girls who have thought that being asked to dress up as a cowgirl was the prelude to some pretty hot action, only to be proved right in quite the wrong way, finding themselves being tied to a stake in the garden and surrounded by the makings of a very serious bonfire.

If you do get an Aries man to leave his toy soldiers alone long enough for you to get him into bed, your problems may not yet be over. He's likely to insist on wearing his Nightrider pyjamas and then to produce the Play-Dough at the weirdest times. The Duplessix survey of 1978 revealed that a huge 90 per cent of Aries men remain totally breast-fixated throughout their lives and scarcely any fewer can get to sleep without there being a light on outside their bedroom. Aries men say prayers for their teddy bears and their favourite footballers before they get into bed. They dribble on the pillow and cry when they have nightmares. Frankly, the *Nannie's Handbook* is likely to be much more useful to the lover of the Aries than *The Perfumed Garden*, and unless you're the kind of woman turned on by a totally maternal role, you should avoid this man like the plague.

Women

A lot of men see the Arietan woman, at twenty-five years of age, buttoned up tight in her flannelette nightdress, sitting in front of the television set with a mug of Ovaltine and gurgling with joy at *Black Beauty*. These same men begin to get some very imaginative ideas about what they would do if only they could get her on her own. Yet how often they are disappointed! For the Aries woman is not the pliable innocent she appears, but a mischievous and super selfish little schemer. There is usually only one way round her pouting petulance, and it's nothing to do with physical prowess – only a Rolex Oyster will do. Then and only then might you expect a glimpse of her favours.

In brief, the Aries woman is made almost exclusively for the attentions of a special kind of roué.

If you are

a) at least twenty years older than her
b) prepared to shower her with endless gifts and trinkets
c) prepared to wear paper hats and ask waiters to bring indoor fireworks instead of liqueurs
d) prepared then to spoon-feed your date

you could be the kind of man who is going to enjoy sex with an Aries woman. Anybody else is going to find the experience one they will never for a moment regret having missed.

THE ARIES DRIVER

Aries people make appalling drivers. Some of them refuse ever to graduate from pedal-powered cars and cause terrible trouble on the roads. Put them in a real car and still they make *brmm, brmm* noises at the wheel. They pretend to be American policemen, with a CB mike in one hand and a toy gun in the other. This habit can – and does – lead to accidents. Even when they own good cars, they have them painted red and white like the one in *Starsky and Hutch* or covered in confederate flags like the one in *Dukes of Hazzard*.

Then, of course, they have to go out and *do* it. They never realize that their favourite heroes use doubles and stunt men. Pausing only to change into their Batman uniforms, they rush outside to try flying the car over the nearest ravine in pursuit of foreign agents or super-criminals.

If you're a driver, an Aries person may be the last

thing you ever see: coming at you out of the sky, A-Team machine gun blazing, Batarang at the ready, and above the whine of the careering car, the last sound you ever hear – a Postman Pat cassette in endless repetition on the hi-fi in the car hurtling towards you. It's enough to make a good Virgoan into an agoraphobic.

LET'S DRESS ARIES

Men

Honestly, the old joke about Aries and nappies is not altogether an exaggeration. On Sunday afternoons in the stockbroker belt, you really can see them padding around a centrally heated mansion dressed in nothing but giant-sized Pampers, sucking gin and tonic from a bottle with a teat. Others will be upstairs in Boy Scout uniforms, playing with their train sets.

These are hardline cases, of course – reminiscent of the Aries man who went into hospital and tried to turn a nurse's head through 360 degrees in the belief that she was a large-size Cindy doll – and usually you have to look a little harder to spot an Aries on the street.

What to look out for? Sensible clothes for a start. An Aries prefers his mother to buy his outfits for him – Clark's shoes, preferably with a compass in a hidden compartment in the heel, grey trousers, Marks and Spencer pullovers, and in winter a nice warm duffel coat with a matching set of bobble hat, scarf and mittens.

Aries men are basically a tailor's nightmare, having no sense of style or class and often the most expensive thing in their wardrobe will be their SAS outfit from Hamley's or their Wyatt Earp gunslinger belt. Try not to be seen with one of these men except at a fancy-dress party.

Women

Unlike Aries men, the women enjoy clothes and know how to get them. For a while, you can fob her off with clothes for her Cindy doll, but pretty soon she discovers a desperate need for St Laurent cocktail dresses and floor-length furs all of her own. This, of course, is where the sugar-daddy comes in. All Aries women who don't have one of these patient providers (a vast majority, naturally) are fearfully bad-tempered and help to get this star-sign its awful reputation.

The fancy clothes, then, are a top priority, but that doesn't mean the Aries woman is prepared to forsake her old favourites. Waiting for her to show up for a date can be a nerve-wracking experience for the image-conscious man (probably a Capricorn). Either she's going to arrive in the most fabulous designer dress that money can buy, or she's going to waddle up in her favourite red Jemimah Puddleduck wellies, a hockey skirt, Aertex shirt and outgrown school blazer. One can easily understand how many men pick up the wrong kind of signals from this kind of dress sense. But be warned about what psychiatrists are now calling the Arietan gym-slip syndrome . . . and see the Food and Entertaining section for an example of what can happen.

In conclusion, it must be said that the way the Aries woman looks is never less than interesting – which is more than can be said for the way she thinks or speaks.

MY FAVOURITE THINGS: ARIES

Paul Daniels, The Monkees, ginger beer, Shirley Temple, Cliff Richard, Bill and Ben, *The Wind in the*

Willows, Michael Jackson, John McEnroe, Disneyland, *Just 17* magazine, Torchy the Battery Boy, Mr T, Roland Rat, pocket video games, Captain Sensible, Mickey Rooney, 'Blue Peter', Christmas pantos, BMX bikes, Jackson Pollock, Ozzy Osborne, Babycham, Mothercare, executive denture caddies, *Ant and Bee Go Shopping*, Manudo, *Bambi*, 'Kid' Jensen.

YOUR GUIDE TO LOVE: ARIES

Aries–Aries
Mars/Mars, Fire/Fire might look good at first, especially when you find your partner just crazy to hang out at the toyshop with you and even play doctor and nurse, but it's clearly going to end in tears. Who's going to cook? Who's going to get anything done? Not you, and not your Aries partner either.

Aries–Taurus
Venus may be the ruling planet of Taurus, but lasting love is an unlikely outcome of this pairing. Simply, your Taurus target is far too dull and conventional to relish your juvenile behaviour.

Aries–Gemini
You reckon you're pretty good at getting your own way, but Gemini is a character who is more than useful at getting other people's goods. If you have anything more valuable than a teddy bear, watch out. Your only possible attraction for a Gemini is your exploitation potential. Love? No way!

Aries–Cancer
The Zodiac chart shows this relationship could have some possibilities – you could play with your Cancer's

microcomputer, for example, but on the whole your Crabby partner is never going to be strong enough to look after your many and various needs.

Aries–Leo
The Sun cuts across Mars and eclipses it. Leos are, if anything, even more self-centred than you are, and entirely unlikely to care about you at all. If you have the fortune to be good-looking (and a terrifyingly high percentage of Arietans are not) a Leo might like to show you off at parties, but probably won't want to bring you home.

Aries–Virgo
The constellations cannot condone this link-up at all. You enjoyed living at home, but must admit your parents could be annoying sometimes. Well, a bitter, fastidious little Virgo is going to be a dozen times worse. Forget about mud-pies! Forget about jam-and-banana sandwiches! Your Virgo lover thinks it's all so *unhealthy*.

Aries–Libra
This one very much depends on the marginal influence of Jupiter at the time of birth. Librans are sadly indecisive people, but may on occasion be just stupid enough to take someone like you in hand. However, with Jupiter on the other side of the chart, they could decide (eventually) to hate you even more than everyone else does.

Aries–Scorpio
Even in terms of paper and ink one hesitates to put these two together! An Aries looks to a Scorpio like a lamb does to a wolf. These twisted, utterly ruthless

individuals have probably only ever prayed once or twice in their nasty lives. And then they prayed for someone like you, *baby*.

Aries–Sagittarius
With Jupiter going straight past Mars here, a romance can hardly be recommended. Sagittarians tend to be clumsy brutes and you would be trampled under foot in their boisterous enthusiasms.

Aries–Capricorn
Let's make no bones about it, Aries. Capricorn is a cruel social climber who won't be interested in you or your dolly-mixtures unless there is something to be gained. So be very careful when one of this lot offers to take you to the zoo or read you a bedtime story. It can't last.

Aries–Aquarius
Whichever way you look at it, self-sufficiency is never going to be your strong suit, and it is a preoccupation of the Aquarian. Still, Air/Fire isn't too bad a mixture and you might just prevail upon the Aquarian's abiding weakness of character to look after you.

Aries–Pisces
Holy Zodiacs! Could there be a more totally wet two-some than you and Pisces? One of the only inspiring things about your natal chart is your dominant element of Fire. Predictably, the spineless Pisces is ruled by water. Any attachment will cancel itself out in apathy, inability and sheer, dithering helplessness.

ARIES FOOD AND ENTERTAINING

Most Aries people have never really outgrown their love of puréed apple and other such baby food that they received in the best years of their life – namely the first two. Ice-cream and lemonade remain great favourites, often to the embarrassment of friends and family. The tale is often told in astrological circles of the elegant, suave and confident Capricorn who was wining and dining a very beautiful young Arietan woman, with the simplest and most foul motives. Being typical of his selfish Sun Sign, the Capricorn ordered the meal for both of them. The consommé was fine – cold and fairly tasteless food being familiar to the blonde-haired beauty with the high-chair mentality – but the Boeuf Wellington was altogether different. She asked him to cut it up for her. The Capricorn, driven wild by the depraved potential of an evening in the company of one so malleable (as he thought) that she even wanted him actually to feed her, lurched across the table and smothered her in kisses. At which entirely unexpected outburst, the gorgeous Arietan stabbed her would-be lover repeatedly and left the restaurant in tears, sucking her thumb.

Here then, for what it's worth, is what you're looking at, at an Aries party.

Starter:
Purée of prunes Tin Tin
(served with crisps and ginger beer)

Fish Course:
Captain Bird's Eye economy fish fingers
(with ketchup)

Main Course:
Mashed potato, gravy, sandwich spread and baked beans
(served with 'soldiers' of bread and butter and a refusal to bring puddings until at least some have been eaten)

Pudding:
Strawberry jelly, ice cream, chocolate sauce, Instant Whip

ARIES ON HOLIDAY

Holidays are no problem for the (remarkably few) rich Arietans. See them at the airport, happily checking into the 'unaccompanied children' lounge, safe in the knowledge that for a handsome fee, someone else is going to take care of everything.

For the poorer dwellers in this first house of the Zodiac, the vacation is going to be more difficult. Camping has a certain appeal. Quite a lot of Aries adults already have the habit of commandeering their children's tents and sleeping in the garden, so that they can have midnight feasts and read old copies of *Parade* by torchlight.

But also popular is the holiday camp. Aries people find it reassuring to have so many mindless entertainments laid on for them. Fellow holidaymakers, of course, must avoid getting caught up in conversation with an Arietan at any time, in case they get trapped into spending the next couple of weeks making sandcastles while everyone else is enjoying the bacchanalian delights of the bar and the disco.

THE ARIES EMPLOYER

Obviously, as employers, these people can be very dangerous indeed. Their care for other people is just minimal, unless they want something from them when their fawning and totally transparent flattery becomes overwhelming. Basically, they cannot conceive of anyone else's life except in so far as it impinges on their own. Aries employers will make you clean their cars, probably with your own clothes. They are the kind of people who will go out at lunchtime and buy a new game, then make you play all afternoon – and woe betide you if you win. In one case, an Aries boss bought a crossbow – ostensibly for his son, but really, as usual, for himself. When he sent his secretary out to buy a pound of apples, she was fortunately intelligent enough to guess the next step (having seen the opera *William Tell* several times with a Leo boyfriend) and ran away, never to return. The boss contented himself with shooting at pigeons from his office window.

Very few people need work so badly that they must work for an Aries employer.

THE ARIES EMPLOYEE

Nobody likes working with an Aries person. Very occasionally an Aries employee can go quite a long way in business by using tantrums, sulks and childish treachery, but more often than not, Aries types are as good as useless – particularly if you are running a toy or ice-cream factory. They cannot be trusted to do anything on their own, even requiring supervision when crossing the road or going to the lavatory. Conscious only of themselves, Aries people make hopeless team players. Most employers find that physical pain is the only thing to which the Aries will respond but the rise of trade union power and the strengthening of industrial legislation has made caning and electric shock treatment increasingly rare as management tools, paradoxically rendering the Aries personality all but unemployable.

YOUR SUN-CYCLE DIARY: ARIES – March 21st–April 20th

March 21st
The first day in your sun cycle. With Mars high in the constellation and no other planetary interference you decide to celebrate by emptying your breakfast over your head. Before dressing for work your partner gives you a good smacking. Perversely you find yourself enjoying it. On the tube travelling to work you pick Milupa from your hair and read the 'ABC of Things'.

March 22nd
With Mars descending and a rampant Virgo in ascendant, the stars predict financial trouble. Forgetting to go to work you spend an anxious day rattling your piggy bank.

March 23rd
The stars in turmoil, with all the elements conspiring against you. Declining to use the tube you travel to work on your plastic Fisher-Price push-kart. Whilst parking you wave at the Managing Director. He looks puzzled and angry and declines to accept your invitation to spend the lunchbreak on the neighbouring

adventure playground. Later in the afternoon he asks you into his office and tells you that there is an interesting position going as paperclip supplies manager in the Biscuit Department. Would you be interested? He asks you to think about it.

March 28th
There is a mutable quality to your stars and life over recent times. The Biscuit Department has its assets – the Krumb-Krispies are delicious – but you miss the thrilling lifestyle you enjoyed in Condiment Despatch.

March 30th
A heavy weekend ahead explaining to your lover that along with your job relocation you have just discovered that your salary has also been relocated to an amount involving fewer figures. Your explanation that fewer figures mean that 'the sums are easier to work out' meets with something less than total approval.

April 4th
Jupiter, Neptune and Mars pass through their own constellations during the coming weeks and spell out a big message: massive changes in (a) your working life; (b) your home life.

April 5th
There is a major reshuffle at work. You've been given the newly created position of assistant carpet cleaner, Executive Division. The Finance Director tells you your salary has been 'rounded off' to an easily understood figure of £100 per annum with a monthly Smarties allowance of 26p. You throw a tantrum and tell him you far prefer Jelly Babies. That evening your partner is

openly unsympathetic when it's time to tuck you into bed.

April 9th
Intergalactic activity on a major scale. Be very cautious and steel yourself for domestic changes.

April 14th
Your partner tells you she is sick of changing nappies for a grown man. She doesn't want to visit the Safari Park any more. She's tired of pushing you round in a pram. Laughing, she tells you she doesn't want to see you again – ever.

April 20th
The last day in your sun cycle – and quite possibly your last day ever. Unable to cook for yourself – unable to even open a can – you are now extremely hungry and are suffering from advanced nappy rash.

GARD
ÉTE
TAURUS JAM
TAURUS JAM
TAURUS JAM
60
RUS JAM
URUS JAM
TAURUS JAM
TAURUS JAM
60
URUS JAM

TAURUS

April 21st–May 21st

'Twixt the horns lies a space'

Old Cretan saying

It is said that Taureans are determined, quiet and dogged characters with a reliable and sane outlook on life. The ideal Taurean male is an airline pilot, bank clerk or gynaecologist – a man who can be relied upon to fulfil his job within the limits of the rule book and no further. The female Taurean has the reputation of being strongly maternal: a coper who draws on her goodness and selflessness to deal with the everyday problems of life.

Well and good the world says, well and good – but the world also has to say that Taureans are the most conventional and boring people in the constellation. The staggering dullness and lack of adventure of these characters beggars description. However there is a deep vein of frustration running through the Taurean character (remember both Pluto and Saturn passed through the Taurean nascence) – Taureans secretly envy people who live glamorous and exciting lives. Exotic, depraved Scorpios, criminal Geminis, snobbish socialite Capricorns are all the apple of the Taurean's eye. This frustration with their own lack of adventure and personal freedom surfaces occasionally in fits of extreme anger. Taurus is a negative fixed earth sign. Very negative.

THE TAURUS MAN

If you meet a man who proves rather quickly to be an extremely boring person, likely as not he'll be a Taurean. There's an irritating smugness to the Taurean male – a smugness born from decades of living in surburbia, wearing Hush Puppies and reading the *Daily Telegraph*. Within minutes he'll be droning on to you about how Mrs Thatcher should be running the NUM, why there are too many blacks in Droitwich and the state of the greens at his golf club. Taurus males have no style and little interest in anyone other than themselves. A high percentage of TV weathermen and driving instructors are Taureans, as are the pinstriped clones who work in the City.

The bearded man in the pub with a pot belly and a CAMRA badge droning on about pork scratchings and real ale is virtually certain to be a Taurean. Quite often his pub acquaintances get so bored with him they'll set him up as a dartboard; but the Taurean male isn't deterred – he is so smug, so certain he is being entertaining, that he's impervious to the darts thudding into him.

THE TAURUS WOMAN

There are two distinctive types of Taurean women. The first is the Earth Mother: an ox-like gargantuan figure striding heartily through Natural Childbirth seminars and the like. The other type is the strapping country lady, a devotee of fêtes, dogs, and making jams. She is likely to wear sensible shoes and skirts made of extremely coarse unfeminine material.

The ruling planet here is Venus so it follows that Taurean women have greedy appetites for small men (watch out Pisceans, Virgoans and Librans).

TAURUS SEX

MEN

The bull is hardly a subtle beast, and it follows that the Taurean male is an outrageously dull and selfish lover, blissfully unaware that women are actually supposed to get pleasure from sex as well (remember Mercury, Mars and Venus all exert strong influences on this sign). The foreplay of a Taurean male can last anything up to five seconds, after which the whole show is over in minutes and he's fast asleep, leaving the object of his attentions wondering when he swallowed the Mogadon.

WOMEN

Taurean women have voracious sexual appetites. This lady is *always* hungry. Johannes Wotan, the pre-eminent German sexologist, offers a theory that a majority of normally sized men can actually survive sex with Taurean women, but the odds on survival for small men are considerably lower. In astrological terms this consequently rules out Piscean, Libran and Virgoan males from entertaining hopes of sexual relations with Taurean women. For the rest there can be real problems if you are (a) on the cusp of Jupiter; (b) in the descendant. Taurean females usually relate badly to (a) and get hysterical about (b).

THE TAURUS DRIVER

Taurus people drive extremely lacklustre vehicles – Austin Maxis, Vauxhall Chevettes, Volvos etc. They are the sort of utterly predictable people who passed their driving test first time and let everybody know about it. They like the 'Mr or Mrs Reliable' image, and so will often be seen driving at 30 mph along motorways on Sunday afternoons, always applying the handbrake on the level, and are almost certain to belong to the AA or RAC – possibly both.

However, don't forget that old Taurean temper. The world's largest traffic jam occurred outside New York City in 1967 – 36,000 cars were tailgated for three days in high summer. US patrolmen ultimately detained several hundred drivers for violent assault on fellow motorists. A State Department report later confirmed the astonishing fact that 92 per cent of those detained were Taureans.

LET'S DRESS TAURUS

Men

Hepworths, Dunn & Co. and Burtons are all ultimate clothing sanctuaries for the Taurus male, who is a certainty for shapeless tweed jackets, pinstripe suits, Viyella checked shirts and Hush Puppies. Taurean males are probably the only people in the world who still insist on wearing vests.

Women

This larger than life figure can go all out for the voluptuous Earth Mother look – i.e. sandals, Guatemalan peasant dress, beads etc., or will look almost exactly like the Taurean male – tweed skirts, lace-up shoes, no-nonsense underwear and maybe a whalebone corset thrown in for luck to support the towering superstructure out front.

MY FAVOURITE THINGS: TAURUS

'Crossroads', Richard Baker, Bismarck, *The Sound of Music*, Gideon's Bible, Robert Redford, Pearl Carr and Teddy Johnson, Hermann Goering, Director's Bitter, Darts, Mary Whitehouse, AA Books, Tony Bennett, *Daily Telegraph*, string vests, Donald Duck, Bing Crosby, *The Mousetrap*, The Seekers, Robert Dougal, Senator Joe McCarthy, Chas 'n' Dave, *Golfer's Weekly*, *Love Story*, Dennis Thatcher, Melanie, Austin Maxis, cavalry twill, Anita Bryant, His 'n' Hers toilet seat covers, 'Tie a Yellow Ribbon', everything about the British Royal Family, *Country Life*, Terry Wogan.

YOUR GUIDE TO LOVE: TAURUS

Taurus–Aries
You are a great conformist by nature, though when pressed are given to irrational rages. Your Aries partner is both irrational and childish so it doesn't take someone like you (who isn't particularly bright) too long to realize this relationship is a cosmic no-no.

Taurus–Taurus
This relationship will have a deeply suburban feel to it. You'll stick together in all probability, because what is known to a Taurean is infinitely better than the unknown. The relationship will finally develop into all

you've ever really wanted from romance – a pleasingly dull and lacklustre affair.

Taurus–Gemini
It's just fight-fight-fight all the way with your Gemini partner in this ghastly Earth/Gas/Air/Malibu partnership. Taureans need to be stimulated into anger more than you'd think and here's just the right kind of dodgy individual who'll satisfy that inner craving.

Taurus–Cancer
You've settled down with one of life's losers. Congratulations! Cancerians offer fantastic benefits to their partners, not least of which is that you should get your own boring way most of the time.

Taurus–Leo
A Venus/Sun pairing. You will find yourself deeply upset by your partner's wish to show off at all times, and by his/her total lack of concern for you as an individual.

Taurus–Virgo
The Earth/Earth combo works as well as you would expect. Both of you have a yearning for order and neatness. After a while you find yourself admiring your obsessively clean little partner.

Taurus–Libra
A Venus/Venus combination, but don't let that fool you. For on thing, Librans have really bad dandruff and for another they just can't decide what to do. If you intend staying with your Libran partner, why don't you make it a lifetime project to get Head and Shoulders on to your loved one's shopping list?

Taurus–Scorpio
Scorpio's a real class manipulator – make no mistake, Taurus. This could be a long-term relationship if you play your cards carefully and do everything your partner wants – or it could be a very short-lived one as your Scorpio partner will have no qualms about getting rid of you. Permanently.

Taurus–Sagittarius
Sagittarians are usually rather stupid people, with an almost Cro Magnon intelligence if Saturn collided with Jupiter on their birthday. So even *you* will have no difficulty in manipulating this person into an ideally conformist partner.

Taurus–Capricorn
Capricorns are natural exploiters and if not naturally clever, are certainly quite cunning. On an intellectual basis there's a hopeless imbalance here, as your average Taurean (and you are pretty average aren't you?) is still wrestling with the concept of the wheel.

Taurus–Aquarius
Aquarians pride themselves on being different. Different could mean anything from knitting wholemeal curtains to starting Camden's first rickshaw cab company. Whatever, it simply doesn't fit into your conception of how the world should be – a place where people behave predictably.

Taurus–Pisces
You are so boring and unadventurous you need next to no stimulation from your partner, but even you draw the line here with this appalling creature from the Jupiter/Neptune constellation.

TAURUS FOOD AND ENTERTAINING

This is the fat person's sign. Taurus people are just plain greedy. They are the type of person who is certain to guzzle several of their favourite chocolates before handing the box around.

If you are unfortunate enough to have a Taurean guest in your home you are going to have a great deal of your food consumed openly in front of you or sneakily from your larder in the early hours. After a while you'll want to be rather nasty to this person from the noxious Venus/Earth/Gas constellation, so why not lay on a surprise party for your guest? While you and your handpicked crowd of professionally unpleasant people (like Capricorns and Scorpios) tuck into an enormous roasted boar, serve your Taurean guest the following meal:

First Course:
One diced cauliflower stalk

Main Course:
Glacé à l'eau (sounds good but looks just like an ice cube. It *is* an ice cube.)

Cheese:
Ecuadorian mule cheese (empty plate served up here – they don't have mules in Ecuador)

Beverage:
Water

TAURUS ON HOLIDAY

Taurus people take their holidays seriously. They have to because everybody else does. South coast resort towns like Bournemouth and Swanage are ideal places for the elderly Taurean to spend his/her holiday. There's something pleasantly dull about these places that appeals to Taureans and they are comforted because everybody around them is certain to (a) be reading the *Daily Telegraph* and (b) think foreigners are peculiar.

Younger Taureans often go to the Club Mediterranée – a conventional unconventionality if ever there was one. One of the main attractions here is that you all live in identical little straw beach huts and can eat unlimited amounts of food.

THE TAURUS EMPLOYER

The Taurus employer is always going to quote the company rule book to you chapter and verse, and has usually been with the firm since the age of five. He is a highly unimaginative and unpopular person who has no leadership skills to speak of and a finely developed sense of his own preservation in the corporate jungle.

THE TAURUS EMPLOYEE

An utterly slavish individual this, who will constantly wear the company tie, has no character of his own, keeps shoe-cleaning equipment in his desk, laughs uproariously at all of the Chairman's jokes, and is heartily despised by all and sundry.

YOUR SUN/CYCLE DIARY: TAURUS – APRIL 21st–MAY 21st

April 21st
The arrangement of the stars suggests that there's

plenty of excitement in store for you over the next few weeks. Expect changes in your professional and personal life.

April 26th
A Gemini moon in the ascendant spells frantic activity at the bank where you work. A day spent nervously awaiting the development of a major internal reshuffle of clerical staff.

April 29th
The bank manager informs you that your most secret wish is now fulfilled – you have made it to bank teller and have now got your own till!

April 30th
With Mars and the prospect of a higher salary exerting a strong influence, you decide to lash out on a new suit from Hepworths. But be careful and beware of a malignant interplanetary conjugation emerging from Saturn and Uranus.

May 4th
A Mercury/Saturn/Uranus triumvirate indicates that you will inevitably forget to put on your underpants today. Later, on the way to work, while pretending to be Roger Moore, your new suit trousers split whilst jumping on to a moving bus. As luck would have it your trousers disintegrate in front of six hysterical Carmelite nuns who insist on an indecent exposure charge. At the station you are given a pair of oversized policeman's trousers with no belt. Smirking, the Duty Sergeant books you for 48 hours.

May 5th

Annoyed by your protestations of innocence, the policeman who is escorting you to the canteen helps you down a twelve-foot flight of steps faster than you expected, and decides to tip off the local press on a good story.

May 6th

The day of your release from prison. However, your jubilation is shortlived when you spot the banner headline 'Bank Man in Carmelite Sex Bus Romp'.

May 7th

You finally get back to work. Immediately you are summoned to see the bank manager. He tells you that the image of a sex maniac with a predilection for exposing himself to nuns and also a police record, is hardly the image that the bank would like its employees to have.

May 12th

After several days' careful thought and a series of uncomfortable interviews with persistent journalists from the tabloid newspapers, the bank manager informs you that you are now an ex-employee.

GEMINI WAS HERE

GEMINI

May 22nd–June 21st

'Beware the mask of Janus, behind it lie two faces and neither of them true'

Francis Bacon

Geminians are versatile, clever and charming people. They are popular for their wit, their quick grasp of situations and their ability to charm the most awkward types. They are successful and are used to being admired by the likes of me and you who – quite simply – don't have any of the qualities of these godlike figures. By hook or by crook Geminians are going to make it to the top of the pile.

In fact these Mercury people sometimes do get there but it is more likely to have been by crook than hook. Geminians are above all deeply criminal. This sign of the twins also reveals a major duplicity (or in other words schizophrenia). Their reputation for wit is based on an inbred ability to lie and their reputation for cleverness on the fact that they are rarely caught out. Right at the top level the ideal Gemini schizo could be flogging malfunctioning atomic weaponry to the Libyans whilst overseeing his parish in Norfolk, or running an international counterfeiting operation whilst holding down a top job at the Royal Mint. Round about the middle of the ladder he/she could be laundering for the Mafia, whilst maintaining a high profile in local Conservative government; while right at the bottom (and remember this is *really* where most Geminians are at) they're to be found evading fares on public transport by pretending to be under age, levering off hubcups, stealing milk from doorsteps by dressing up as milk-men, and robbing old age pensioners by posing as meter readers. Don't play cards with these people – they will cheat you to kingdom come.

THE GEMINI MAN

Many people have remarked how shifty-eyed Gemini men can be: they never look you in the eye for long. As he stands to the side of you at the party – his eyes flickering across the room – he will, likely as not, be trying to sell you something – insurance probably or even a De Lorean car.

Geminians are natural salesmen. This Third House of the Zodiac contains many conflicting elements not least of which is the ability to cheat other people. Geminians are two-faced and will use this characteristic to full advantage when they prey on others. Natural suckers for Gemini sales techniques are Pisceans who are persuaded to buy a pair of right-footed moonboots when going on holiday to the South of France, or Capricorns who will be coerced into buying a fake Dukedom, and of course Leos whose acquisitiveness will force them to purchase – say – a pair of diamanté shoehorns or something similarly tasteful.

THE GEMINI WOMAN

At some point in their lives nearly everyone has been taken in by a Gemini woman. She seems so pleasant and quick-witted, so understanding and appreciative. It's only when you notice some little thing missing from the house – your wallet, for example – that you begin to get an inkling of what the word 'mercurial' really means.

Gemini women give the rest of their sex a bad name. They are cheats who use every kind of wile to get their own way. Like all people born beneath this two-faced sign, they are pathological liars, so gauging their true emotions is almost impossible. They often have well-stocked kitchens since they make adept shoplifters, but they are not great home-makers, since left on their own in the home they have no one to rob but themselves. On the other hand, their low cunning can lead to big success in business. They make good saleswomen, with an excellent line in customer-flattery, and staying on the right side in office politics comes naturally to them. They have no sense of loyalty and no concept of trust.

They have a reputation for being charming hostesses and they often do a lot of their charming on a one-to-one basis upstairs which can leave the rest of the dinner party feeling rather embarrassed. Gemini women tend to use huge quantities of make-up and hair dye.

GEMINI SEX

Men

Many women have reported a profound disappointment with Gemini males. Like all those born to the Third House of the Zodiac, the Gemini man is a great talker. However, when the talking has to stop, his conversational ability is not always matched by his physical performance. Put very bluntly, a lot of Gemini men are impotent.

What can you do? Well, don't try urging your new lover to a satisfactory state of excitement by pulling out the old kinky handcuffs – that may work for a Libran or a Cancerian, but your Geminian is likely to dive straight out of the window! Also, you should be tolerant if your Gemini date appears to have forgotten what to do in bed. He's very probably just spent a long time in a place where there are no women.

Still, let's not get too sympathetic. After all, this man is probably only sleeping with you because it's an easier way of getting into the house than jemmying open the back door later on. Leave the light on and try to stay awake. From that point of view, at least, you can be thankful that the Gemini lover is so inadequate – he's hardly going to tire you out. Watch for when he takes his shades off . . .

Women

Some cynics suggests that the only difference between sex with a Capricorn woman and sex with a Gemini woman is that the Capricorn does at least pretend to be enjoying the whole business (and business it certainly is for these girls). But this is surely unfair to the Geminians, some of whom can produce remarkable displays of affection when the chips are down. They can get really passionate towards men who wear keys dangling from their belts, for example, particularly bank managers and prison warders. In fact psychiatrists have proved almost beyond doubt that the fake orgasm was invented by Gemini women. Some Gemini women can't actually tell the difference between a fake orgasm and a real one. However they do fool a lot of men and it usually takes someone as deceitful and unpleasant as, say, a Capricorn, to realize that it's just an act. A popular trick that is mean but amusing is to whisper into the Gemini lover's ear at the moment of ecstasy something like 'What's 19 times £23.41p?' Almost every time she'll flash back the answer without even resorting to the built-in calculator on the bed head.

THE GEMINI DRIVER

Geminians are extremely car conscious, and above all signs – even Leo – are pathetically aware of the car as a status symbol.

Very rich, very crooked Geminians enjoy driving top-of-the-line models with unique features, e.g. Maserati with ludicrous turbo-charged seat adjusters. Young Gemini crooks-about-town will aspire to a white Escort XR3. Aspire is the right word because most of them drive little Hondas with pathetic transfers on the rear window like 'Don't laugh, your daughter might be inside!' There's nothing like hoping.

LET'S DRESS GEMINI

Men

Gemini men can be seen wearing ill-fitting suits made of sackcloth, with arrows all over them. Yes, they're prison uniforms! – no, *seriously*, Gemini men (when they're out or on parole) are really sharp dressers. They enjoy wearing sunglasses at night in winter; they will probably still own a pair of stone-washed flared jeans. They might even have a shirt or two from Van Heusen!!

Women

Above all a Gemini woman will like to think of herself as being (a) supercool, (b) supersophisticated, and (c) in business. This means that she will wear big red glasses and always carry a thin briefcase (even when having a shower). On Saturdays she can be seen wearing big floppy T-shirts with 'Frankie Does Things to a Goat' written on the front in BIG LETTERS.

MY FAVOURITE THINGS: GEMINI

Richard Nixon, John Poulson, 'Delilah', wide lapels, Ronnie and Reggie Kray, Cecil Rhodes, brand-name sweaters, Jimmy Hill, Bob Monkhouse, Andrew Lloyd-Webber, Escort XRIs, Shirley Conran, stilettos, sheepskin coats, Spiro T. Agnew, Bernie Cornfeld's, 'Do You Sincerely Want to be Rich?', Barbara Windsor, Janet Street Porter, pointed toe caps, Allen Klein, MFI furniture, Lionel Ritchie, table nests, Al Capone, King Richard III, Alex 'Hurricane' Higgins, Tom Keating, *The Great Train Robbery*, Frank Sinatra, Las Vegas, whitewall tyres, John Francome.

YOUR GUIDE TO LOVE: GEMINI

Gemini–Aries
A wildly unorthodox combination this – and make no mistake! You're ruled by Air and Aries by Wind – so watch out for gale warnings! Arietans have the perception of children and will ask you embarrassing questions in front of people you are trying to impress, e.g. 'What's the food like in Wormwood Scrubs?'

Gemini–Taurus
You're unconventional and – let's face it – no stranger to dishonesty, while your Taurean partner is extremely

conventional and dull, but can be relied upon to always arrive in time for visiting hour at the prison. Bear this in mind, Gemini.

Gemini–Gemini
A good relationship is based on trust so no prizes for guessing that this one is going to have its problems. The classic Mercury/Mercury partnership can only begin to work if there have been both fixed planetary and mutable aspects in the nativity – and we all know that that is virtually an astrological impossibility.

Gemini–Cancer
You're pretty selfish given the chance – and here's the kind of insignificant chance you've been dreaming about for years. This is someone who will cling desperately to you however, particularly when you wish (as you will wish) to terminate the relationship.

Gemini–Leo
Selling is your life and here is your perfect partner – a gross materialist who loves to buy. Your elemental conjunction of Air and Fire will offer you complicity, harmony and good commission percentages.

Gemini–Virgo
If you consider laughter to be an important part of life you'd be well advised to give this Sign a wide berth. Furthermore Virgo's innate suspicion might well suss out your criminal tendencies. Proceed with extreme caution into this unholy Mercury/Mercury Air/Earth match.

Gemini–Libra
Does your Libran love you? Yes . . . and no. The truth is Librans can't decide. You rate yourself as being a

pretty decisive type – but do you really think you could tolerate a total opposite, particularly if both Venus and Jupiter were ascending at the same time?

Gemini–Scorpio
The Air/Water combination looks good on paper . . . but a single lapse of concentration could see this ruthless personality walking all over you.

Gemini–Sagittarius
It may be blissful at first, realizing you can cheat at will on somebody who is extremely stupid. But after forty years the thrill will wear off. There is a poor planetary conjunction here.

Gemini–Capricorn
You are both liars and thieves – but your Capricorn partner is likely to be a whole lot smarter and more sophisticated than you are. Your loved one will be embarrassed when you try to sell a second-hand Ford Capri to a member of the Royal Family at Ascot. Thinking about it afterwards even you will be embarrassed.

Gemini–Aquarius
If you think somebody this weak and pliable is going to be fun to live with, watch out! You are going to be annoyed by this person. You used to enjoy watching *The Professionals*, eating Big Macs, listening to a few old Slade hits. Now your Aquarian partner has welded the TV selector button on to Channel 4, you eat soya-bean yoghourts, and your freaky friend is threatening to knit you some macrobiotic socks.

Gemini–Pisces
Here's a character (for want of a better word) who will be pathetically grateful to be even spoken to – let alone

lived with. But the question remains – why bother?

GEMINI FOOD AND ENTERTAINING

Geminians like to impress people with their sophisticated ways. A rich Gemini host will prepare a sumptuous feast for his guests, yet wreck it by offering cherry brandy with the soup. He is the sort of person who will openly search around in his mouth for bits of meat lodged in his teeth. Here is the gorgeous Gemini repast:

Starter:
Pâté de Foie Gras – served with Watney's Red Barrel and/or Coca-Cola

Main Course:
Ol Ma Debakey's baked Taco mix, Mexican chiliburgers, french fries, served with an exquisitely rare Chablis

Pudding:
Spotted Dick, served with 1912 Cognac

GEMINI ON HOLIDAY

Geminians are quite smart, but not quite smart enough. This may mean flying all the way to the Caribbean just in time for the rainy season or zeroing in on St Tropez just when it began to get spoilt.

Naturally Geminis are drawn like moths to internationally famous criminal communities like Southern

Spain. (Ronnie Biggs, an internationally famous Geminian, decided to take his holiday in Brazil – permanently.)

THE GEMINI EMPLOYER

Unlikely to be a good boss to work for, the Gemini employer will have a lot of fun spending your wages and then lying about what happened to them. Their fundamentally split personality makes Geminians hell to be with in the office. One minute they'll be patting you on the back, the next you're fired for wearing the wrong colour socks. Try to steer well clear if you can.

THE GEMINI EMPLOYEE

Not a good idea, but often hard to avoid. Geminians are congenital liars, so they will rarely tell the truth on application forms. Thus you may not be able to weed them out at this early stage. Geminians are probably the best salesmen in the world, particularly of goods that people don't really want. Never trust a Geminian employee with money – embezzlement is a way of life for them.

YOUR SUN-CYCLE DIARY: GEMINI – MAY 22nd–JUNE 21st

May 22nd
An auspicious start to the third phase of the Zodiac. Your neighbour calls to say he's going on holiday; if he

gives you the keys, could you nip in from time to time and water his plants? With a sickening smile you jump at the chance.

May 24th
Worried about your Aunt Bessie in Bridgetown, Barbados. You have been telephoning her for two days now from your neighbour's flat, and she hasn't replied. Is she on holiday?

May 28th
Saturn rising right across your fixed aspects. Not a good day physically. You hurt your back carrying your neighbour's television set to the pawnbroker and hardly receive enough money to pay for the taxi home.

June 1st
Saturn descending but things looking up. A good day for playing with the credit card you stole from your mother, perhaps.

June 2nd
Should have noticed a bad galactic conjunction as Saturn dipped past Venus. Your mother's credit card was out of date! Sales Assistant at Harrods not amused at having to put everything back on the shelf, but at least you get away in the confusion.

June 4th
A frustrating couple of hours spent trying to open your neighbour's front door with the credit card before you remember he gave you the keys. Once inside, you eat, drink and relax listening to the New York speaking clock for an hour or so.

June 6th
A big bank heist is pulled off downtown and almost immediately the police are on your doorstep. You are rather flattered until you realize they are only making a collection for charity. You manage to slip a penny and three buttons into the tin.

June 8th
Your neighbours return from holiday. Your well-rehearsed performance of horror and outrage should surely merit an Oscar.

June 10th
Problems for Mercury as the quicksilver planet careers across the astral plane. The policeman assigned to the case of your neighbour's burglary has a horrible air of familiarity.

June 11th
The police recover the television set from the pawn-broker. The rest of your neighbour's inventory is now under sheets in your spare bedroom. So far so good.

June 13th
Unlucky for some, extremely unlucky for you, you hurt your foot in trying to kick open a vending machine outside the sweet shop.

June 18th
Foot still hurts. Grudgingly you allow your neighbour to use your phone to call the insurance company. His has been cut off pending the settlement of a four-figure bill.

June 19th
Unexpectedly (with Mars in the house of Uranus) your Aunt from Barbados rings up. She has been on a banana boat for eight weeks and demands a place to stay. Since she cannot use the spare room, you ask your neighbours to put her up.

June 20th
Pluto badly affected by Mercury. A terrible revelation: your Aunt is also a Geminian. You come home from a day spent stealing underwear from washing lines only to find the old bird has broken into your flat and tried to sell your neighbours all their own possessions.

June 21st
Things could be worse. The cells are cool in summer, and the police doctor will operate on your septic foot free of charge. (But the pliers look ominous.)

CANCER

CANCER

June 22nd–July 23rd

'Thou hast scuttled away from all of life's opportunities, and do even now build thy home in sand'

Christopher Marlowe

Cancerians are quiet and self-possessed people, with a strong artistic streak to them. Underneath their pleasant and misleadingly shy nature, lurks a determination to achieve in life. These are Moon people born under the sign of the Crab, and Cancerians have inherited all of the magical beauty and mystery of that planet.

In fact, far from being impressed by their artistry and determination, people who know Cancerians are more impressed by their lack of social graces, their self-righteousness, awful self-pity, irresponsibility and – perhaps above all – the Cancerian's legendary moodiness. A Cancerian's moods are synchronized to the Moon's multi-gravitational pull – so as the Moon swings through its various diurnal equinoxes it follows with a horrible inevitability that your Cancerian aquaintance can burst into tears for no apparent reason, throw a terrible tantrum in a crowded restaurant and start laughing loudly on a visit to the Opera during the death scene in *Madame Butterfly*.

So who wants these people with their wildly changing moods, their terrible manners and dreadful irresponsibility? Short answer: practically no one. Very few people are actively seeking a partner who is a tremendous liability, and who is going to upset other people's feelings continually.

THE CANCER MAN

It is a virtual astrological certainty that this creature is going to have a hobby – possibly several. There is a very real danger that he might show you, with pride, his collection of EEC beer mats, his massive architectural model made from three million pieces of Meccano, or his complete complement of WW II fighter planes made by himself out of balsa wood. Cancer males are tremendously cowardly – virtually the entire Italian army in WW II was made up of Crab people.

Above all else though, the Cancer male has found his spiritual home in the microcomputer. It is a mystery to most sane people why anyone should actually want to own a micro or attend a microcomputer fair, and even more of a mystery why it is that those who do so are all male, myopic, and dressed ridiculously badly. The answer is simple: they are all Cancer males.

As if the above evidence were not damning enough, it is also worth pointing out that a very high percentage of Scoutmasters are Cancerians.

THE CANCER WOMAN

The Moon is a feminine deity and as goddesses go Cancer females are not among the front runners. They can be rather sly and scheming given half a chance, and *very* emotional. The suitor to the Cancer female may think it's rather charming and tactful to remark (falsely or not) on how beautiful she is looking, after her new hairdo, to be met with a torrent of tears and verbal abuse because this implies her hair looked like an uncut hedge before. Equally the Cancer female might be enjoying an evening of intellectual superiority with a Sagittarian man at some quiet restaurant, when suddenly her mood changes; she's a Fire sign on the ascendant, a raving banshee, a bad night at La Scala. You never quite know how a Cancer female is going to behave and because of this she is frequently given a wide berth. Needless to say she has no sense of humour.

CANCER SEX

Men

Women love challenges and there is no greater challenge known to the female sex than prising a Cancer man away from his model train set or microcomputer, and into bed. They frequently have to resort to bribes like buying him the latest computer fantasy game, or Wayfinder shoes with secret compartments in the heel.

Assuming the bribe works there he is: Mr Dynamism himself. According to Kinsey's detailed statistics compiled over several years, Cancer males make either energetic lovers or complete zeros, occasionally combining both characteristics in one sitting. One minute he's an ape swinging through the jungle of physical intimacy, the next his astonished partner realizes he has lost interest completely and is playing 'Hunt the Quark' on his Commodore 64.

Women

Cancer women fancy themselves as being extremely attractive to the opposite sex. But are they actually? Many men have been perplexed by the Cancerienne's quickly changing moods, which are likely to become pronounced when it comes to matters of the flesh. One minute it's on, the next minute it's off. It is reasonable to conclude that the Cancer woman is a frightful tease.

It takes somebody as desperate as a Sagittarian or a Libran who is going to tolerate this type of behaviour. Often they have to put up with the sulks and tantrums not to mention their own physical frustration, for several years. When their partner has finally been bedded, reports indicate a profound disappointment. What was all the fuss about?

THE CANCER DRIVER

The Cancer driver is a moody and irresponsible beast who can never be depended upon entirely to stop at a red light. They have an alarming crablike tendency to drift sideways across the road, and are equally capable of sauntering along the fast lane of a motorway at 40 mph or treating the North Circular Road as if it were Le Mans.

Most people know they are close to a Cancer driver at the moment of impact. In order to spot them early and take evasive action a couple of tips are offered. Firstly the Cancer car is likely to be a honeycomb of dents, and secondly there is more than likely to be a car sticker saying 'Don't follow me – I'm lost too'. There might even be a nodding dog. Pull off the road fast.

LET'S DRESS CANCER

Men

Cancer men do dress badly. You can identify this person instantly because he wears white socks with dark suits, and shirts that were obviously given away free at garages. Beneath the shirt you can trace the outline of a vest. His tie is so loud it could be seen by a satellite in poor weather.

Male Cancerians frequently wear pens in their top pockets. The person whose digital watch alarm goes off in a hushed cinema is certain to be a Cancer man.

Women

There's no other word for it: these women dress in an *emotional* way. She intends to be noticed, and she *is* – with her yellow Bonaparte cockade hat, her ludicrous luminous Gucci shoes, her handbag made from New Guinea marsupials and her extravagant make-up applied with a trowel.

MY FAVOURITE THINGS: CANCER

General Galtieri, Geoff Boycott, Freddie Mercury, BBC micros, Emperor Nero, John Curry, Noel Edmonds, Dr Crippen, K-Tel Hits, Oswald Mosley, Steven Spielberg, Al Stewart, 'Hunt the Quark' computer games, Gary Gilmour, Dennis Healey, Sir Clive Sinclair, 'The Golden Shot', George III, digital toasters, Neil Young, Little Richard, model aeroplanes, stamp collecting, flying kites, *Star Trek*, Michael Aspel.

YOUR GUIDE TO LOVE: CANCER

Cancer–Aries
Aries are childish and spoilt people who are inclined to shout and scream when they don't get their own way. This Mars/Moon match is fraught with problems, not least because you can be a little like that too when the mood takes you.

Cancer–Taurus
Your fixed astral aspect is Pepsi and Taurus is Gas. What a mixture! However you do have one thing in common – self-righteousness. Beware, this is a characteristic which can lead to intense arguments as you both always think you're in the right.

Cancer–Gemini
On the face of it a not unreasonable partnership, but don't think it's going to be a bowl of cherries, Cancer, as your partner is likely to be spending several years away from you in top security wings.

Cancer–Cancer
Two Cancer people together can be a truly wonderful relationship. You'll have lots of fun spying on each other, arguing, playing with your microcomputers and, occasionally, each other.

Cancer–Leo
Water and Fire. One puts out the other! You'll really have to take the back seat with a Leo around, quite literally as your partner will be so bored with you there'll be somebody else in front.

Cancer–Virgo
Despite your fixed astral aspects of Pepsi and Perrier being total opposites, you do share one common characteristic: you are both awful cowards. However this is not a good basis for a harmonious relationship, as you will find out in due course.

Cancer–Libra
Librans can get irritable if they've half a mind, and they well might have with you around. Therefore proceed into this relationship with extreme caution, since you've never been one for all-in wrestling round the kitchen.

Cancer–Scorpio
You are both Water Signs, but that's where the similarity ends. Astrologically this is a monstrously implausible relationship whose only chance of survival is complete submission by you to all of your Scorpio partner's unreasonable demands.

Cancer–Sagittarius
Sagittarians are the world's meatheads. They are immensely stupid, frivolous and with no mind of their own to speak of. If you can accept an imbalance of intelligence in this pairing then you could be on to something here as you are likely to get your own way the whole time.

Cancer–Capricorn
Capricorns are ambitious social climbers, make no mistake about that. You'll go further in this partnership than you would have otherwise, but your Capricorn mate will sort out the direction you go in. Socially the direction you're going in is Glyndebourne and the City via Ascot. Can you handle it?

Cancer–Aquarius
A Moon/Saturn–Uranus pairing that has more going for it than you would think. Firstly Aquarians are actually quite hung up on being nice to other people, in a sort of dimwitted Vegan way, so you are going to get more sympathy and attention than your miserable character actually deserves. Secondly Aquarians are notoriously bad with money, so you will be able to manipulate that end of things quite nicely.

Cancer–Pisces
Astrologically speaking it's very disappointing to see you've decided to settle with second best. Pisces is very much the bottom rung of the astro ladder. The only thing one can say about this 'relationship' is that you can programme your Pisces partner to do all of the household chores. However you *can* do exciting things together like watching TV or listening to 'The Archers'.

CANCER FOOD AND ENTERTAINING

A Cancer host or hostess can make the dinner party they give a particularly uncomfortable occasion, due to the likelihood that he or she will be in one of their famous moods or sulks. Often the food will be carelessly prepared, and the astonished guests will be treated to a disgusting meal.

Here then is the likely Cancer repast:

Starter:
Oeufs en gelée. By mistake cooked in gelatine not aspic. Absolutely inedible.

Main Course:
Roast chicken. Cooked with polythene bag of giblets left inside. A course of mind-boggling frightfulness.

Pudding:
Cheese. The 'fromages' are so old that they are limbo-dancing across the plate.

Beverage:
Retsina. Guaranteed to give all imbibers a violent headache within minutes.

CANCER ON HOLIDAY

Cancerians on holiday are unpopular with their fellow holidaymakers because they're always complaining about the food, arguing with the tour guide, refusing to join in, and queue-barge at breakfast.

When abroad they show no curiosity about foreigners and are constantly stealing other people's enterovioform. They wear Dr Scholl's shoes on the beach and dislike appearing in group photographs. They buy shabby local artifacts from airport stalls.

THE CANCER EMPLOYER

You need a Cancer boss like you need brain surgery. This is a very disagreeable and sneaky person to work for indeed, who will scheme to get you fired while pretending that you're the best thing since the invention of the wheel.

THE CANCER EMPLOYEE

Cancerians tend to dominate the clerical side of a business and rarely rise higher up the corporate ladder. An employer should beware of the Cancer employee's moods and latent irresponsibility. Crab people don't like to look at things straight on, they prefer a sideways approach.

YOUR SUN-CYCLE DIARY: CANCER – JUNE 22nd–JULY 23rd

June 22nd
With Mars in the ascendant the constellation is conspiring against you; a violent thunderstorm ruins the barbecue you and your loved one had planned.

June 29th
With all the planets, except Venus, ascending rapidly, likely as not you're in for a really punishing time in your private life.

July 1st
The telephone bill arrives revealing several thousand pounds' worth of calls to Australia. You don't know anyone in Australia.

July 3rd
With the diurnal axis tilting away from Venus, you find yourself perplexed and worried by that telephone bill. You can't pay it and you can't understand why there have been so many calls to Australia. A call to the

enquiries office at British Telecom proves to be singularly unhelpful.

July 6th
You have been in a terrible mood for several days now, not helped by your feeling of estrangement from your partner.

July 14th
Anniversary of the outbreak of the Black Death. There are no letters for you but two for your loved one. Curiously both are postmarked Perth, Australia.

July 15th
You still can't find the right opportunity to raise the subject of those letters in conversation.

July 16th
A letter arrives from Qantas.

July 18th
Your loved one has left you. On reflection you realize you were a little slow on the uptake as you watched your loved one pack a large trunk and call a cab to be driven to Heathrow Airport, terminal 3.

July 20th
You visit your parents for some comfort and advice. With Venus re-establishing itself in its previous interstellar position, you are determined to get your life back on the right tracks. In the afternoon you get up to go for a long walk in the garden. Too late, you remember they live in a high-rise flat.

LEO'S ONLY

LEO

July 24th–August 23rd

'He hath neither prudence nor restraint, only a love of gold'

Ben Jonson

Hey, big cat! Extrovert, generous and proud, luxury-loving Leo is someone you will find rising, like cream, into all the important positions in life. A natural leader with the natural grace of the lion, but also with some of the deadlier instincts for survival exhibited by the king of the jungle. The leonine element is Fire, the favoured metal is gold and the ruling planet is the Sun.

Success in all things comes easily to a Leo – including such things as lying and arrogant self-delusion. In fact, the foregoing character-description is the kind of drivel that only a Leo would tell you, or believe. Because Leos, of all the people under the Sun, are the most obnoxious, bossy, unfeeling and ostentatious. Pushy, flashy and greedy, the Leo man or woman may be flattered in public, but is in private almost universally despised. Make that totally. No one but an utter moron (see *Pisces*) has ever liked a Leo for anything other than professional reasons.

Leos have a great love of showing off and luxury which, combined with their natural flair for sheer bad taste, can make living with or near them a tacky experience. Leos are a salesman's delight, since they can easily be flattered into buying almost any circular bath with real gold plated-taps, or living-room bar with studded vinyl in front and pineapple ice bucket on top, or set of encyclopaedias bound in real leather-look kidron. Their homes are not noted for elegant simplicity. Leos are unpleasant people who don't want to be loved so much as envied.

THE LEO MAN

Napoleon Bonaparte was a Leo and Leo men make a lot of this fact. In truth many of them are a lot like that infamous Frenchman: short, bald, megalomaniac, and ultimately unsuccessful. They too spend a lot of time with their hands thrust into their jackets, fondling their gold medallions. Leo is a Fire sign and that generally spells trouble: a fire is something it's hard to ignore, and a Leo will go to any lengths to get noticed. At its simplest, this means turning up at a disco bearing a hundred ounces of gold on various chains and rings; at its most complicated it could mean conquering Europe by force of arms. Either way, it's not going to be any fun for the rest of us.

Leo men frequently compare themselves with people like Burt Reynolds, Bryan Robson and Albert Einstein and usually decide that they survive the comparison rather well. No one is more vain than a Leo man.

THE LEO WOMAN

The Leo woman, meanwhile, also runs true to type. Anybody who really knows anything about lions, will know of course that the male, far from ruling the jungle, merely lolls around scratching his private parts, while the female indulges in her favourite pastime of murdering innocent passers-by. Grabby, vicious and seriously unpleasant, this is indeed the Leo personality made real in the animal kingdom.

Leo women pamper themselves in health spas, spend their husband's money on gigolos, wear costume jewellery in ludicrous amounts, take poodles to restaurants, have face-lifts, breast enlargements, nose-jobs and weekly hairdos; they stare at their reflections in shop windows, they eat huge cream cakes and have conspicuously loose morals.

LEO SEX

Men

It is a cosmic certainty that a Leo can only be in love with a Leo, and that Leo is himself. A Leo cannot bear to have anyone else share the lime-light, particularly in bed. The Leo man tends to be a lover of predictably selfish habits. In fact, when not making love to himself, he may just as well be doing so, for all the satisfaction that his partner is likely to receive from him, but you wouldn't guess it from the press-conference: the Leo man saves his best performance for afterwards, reaching a bizarre kind of post-coital climax in a barrage of interrogatives.

> Wasn't that the best?
> Isn't that the biggest?
> Did the Earth move?
> How far did the Earth move?
> Are you frigid, or what?

By this time, his lover, bruised and battered by the Leo's 'technique' (they say that you can tell a Leo partner by the shape of a gold ingot imprinted in perfect bas-relief on her chest), will be in less than an ecstatic frame of mind, but our determined Leo is the last person in the world to notice. He drifts into a contented and noisy sleep, his super-stud reputation secure still in his own mind, that place where so many of his finest moments have taken place.

Women

The Leo woman is likewise not noted for her bedside manners. She tends to be greedy and demanding. The only consolation for her lovers is that while she may humiliate you in bed – 'that reminds me of a penis, only smaller' – she will probably give you a good press afterwards, since like all Leos, her principal concern is self-promotion. Even a moderately straightforward sexual encounter will later be reported to her 'friends' as toppling houses in Tokyo.

THE LEO DRIVER

Because of their phenomenal conceit and total lack of human sensitivity, Leos are quite frequently successful in business, particularly in America, and therefore they will often be found in expensive cars. As with everything else in their life, of course, they overdo it. The gold Rolls-Royce with real fur seat-covers almost certainly belongs to a Leo, as does the ludicrous Cadillac with a television aerial on the boot. Only a Leo could think that other people would be impressed by a Jaguar XJS painted and supplied in green and gold by Harrods, because only a Leo could be impressed by it in the first place.

But if there is one thing worse than a rich Leo, most people absolutely agree it is a poor Leo. This pathetic creature is a natural show-off with nothing to show off about, an abject materialist with very little material to work with. So watch out for the Morris Minor with wide wheels and go-faster stripes – that's the Leo who can't afford a proper car! You must avoid this creature just as you would avoid, say, a doctor that you knew to be a Scorpio.

LET'S DRESS LEO

Men

The Leo man goes for the richly casual look, and often misses. The man at the funeral with brilliant white suit, unbuttoned black shirt, white shoes and a large cigar is almost certainly a Leo. He only ever wears his fur-collared coat thrown over his shoulders.

Since even Leos draw the line at actually leaving price tags pinned to their sleeve, they have become the principal beneficiaries of, and inspiration for, the boom in clothes with identifiable brand names like Lacoste. Most people, of course, think it is fairly stupid to pay £30 for a £10 shirt merely because it has a little alligator on the front. Not so the Leo! He thinks that little beast is better than money in the bank – because what's the use of money where other people can't see it?

Women

Leo women have no trouble finding clothes. Simply, they can be relied upon to be impeccably overdressed at every occasion. Leos love opulence but have no real taste. If they can possibly pay more than is necessary for something, then they will. Being natural-born show-offs, however, they won't be happy unless everyone else can tell how much they've paid. With the same attitude to brand names as their menfolk, they may as well be walking along with sandwich boards advertising the names of trendy clothes manufacturers. No one ever accused a Leo woman of being too subtle.

Many of them develop elongated arms, like apes, on account of the huge number of rings they wear on their fingers. Leo women favour fur coats (for summer), mini skirts (for winter) and tennis kit (for shopping). They sport too much make-up, not enough underwear and a year-round tan. They are vain beyond imagining.

MY FAVOURITE THINGS: LEO

Jonathan King, Cher, waterbeds, Arnold Schwartzenneger, Boadicea, Tom Jones, Caesar's Palace, Harrods, Liberace, platform heels, coke spoons, Cleopatra, *The Sun*, 'The Lucy Show', Alice Cooper, sideburns, low-cut dresses, costume jewellery, Gary Glitter, Ferraris, Rod Stewart, windsurfing, 'E Viva Espagna', Dave Lee Travis, spandex trousers, elephant foot wastepaper baskets, Fortnums, caviar, T. Rex, gold medallions, diamond dog collars, Raymond's Revue Bar, Ron Atkinson, Napoleon, Bob 'Penthouse' Guccione, Mussolini, 'My Way', multi-coloured contraceptives, Barry Manilow, Tony Blackburn.

YOUR GUIDE TO LOVE: LEO

Leo–Aries
Mars has a big effect here, and it's not for the good.

You want to be a star – so does the infantile Ram. This relationship ain't big enough for both of you.

Leo–Taurus

There have been worse conjunctions, but hitching your star to this Earthy Venusian isn't going to lead to many thrills for you. The hyper-conventional Taurean is going to disapprove of your party clothes and will certainly confiscate your Coke spoon before you go out. You'll be stifled in this relationship.

Leo–Gemini

You will really like your Gemini partner who will flatter your huge ego continually; but be warned. This is the sign of the professional liar. Your famed generosity could be the target!

Leo–Cancer

About the only way you can have fun with a Cancerian is by leaving the little wimp at home. Good idea, Big Cat?

Leo–Leo

Your ideal partner is probably a full-length mirror, but if you want an animate mate then another Leo is not the answer. You couldn't cope with somebody as selfish as yourself.

Leo–Virgo

With Mercury rising you have got to find this a very difficult love match, indeed. You are game for a laugh and fancy free. Your hairdresser friend doesn't know what fun is. Leave it out, Leo!

Leo–Libra
You could help this dithering dodo to decide a few things – like whether you should have your birthday party at the Ritz, the Savoy or (your choice) both. Could do worse than this little character.

Leo–Scorpio
Mars and Pluto power across the Constellation: a Scorpio is not going to be impressed by your arrogant showing off, and may in fact undertake malicious plans to foil your singleminded pursuit of your own happiness.

Leo–Sagittarius
This is possibly the kind of loser you can live with. Jupiter dominates the Sagittarian character, so you will have no problems in leading this partnership. But this meathead is hardly the kind of person you'll want to show off about. And showing off is what you do best, isn't it?

Leo–Capricorn
This unpleasantly ambitious little climber and thief will at least accompany you to all the right parties, even if for all the wrong reasons. Keep an eye on that imitation Rolex you cart around on your wrist: you might find your Capricorn partner sawing your hand off to get it.

Leo–Aquarius
This combination is likely to be a bit too home-baked for your tastes, a little too trendy and SDP for a flagrant capitalist like you. Your extravagance fails to impress at Amnesty International Benefits and the like. What do you do now? Look for a Pisces, of course.

Leo–Pisces
OK, so you can't actually show off about having a Pisces lover, but you can show off *to* this chronically inadequate misfit morning, noon and night. A quick glance at the ruling planets in this combination reveal an enticing triune of Sun/Jupiter/Neptune. So it's all systems go for the lucky Leo – this could be a real winner.

LEO FOOD AND ENTERTAINING

No health foods here. Leos are ostentatious vulgar people who like eating meat with their hands. They have sculptures carved out of ice to sit on their tables. They have larks' tongue sandwiches in their packed lunches so that they can tell everyone else how much they cost. They pour golden syrup on ice cream. They frequently drink warm Nigerian Champagne. They like dining in famous and stupidly over-priced restaurants and do their shopping either at Harrods or in late-night supermarkets, for the sheer joy of spending too much money.

Ideal Menu

Starter:
Caviar (served with price tag)

Main Course:
Roast boar (for the Leo to tear apart and distribute according to the selfish whim of the moment)

Pudding:
Cream

Beverage:
Crème de Menthe

LEO ON HOLIDAY

Leos being, naturally, great followers of the Sun, and bullshit-artists *par excellence*, it is their profoundest ambition, at all times of the year, to be in LA. If they can't get there professionally, then that is where you will find them on holiday – paradoxically wearing a business suit and lugging round a briefcase in order to live up to the futile, illusory image of their own success. Those who can't afford LA usually fetch up in Marbella, pretending to any and every other tourist they can find that they do in fact spend the other fifty weeks of the year in LA. Really serious Leo failures settle for Clacton, sweatily proclaiming on the disco dance-floor that they spend a lot of time in Marbella.

THE LEO EMPLOYER

The Leo employer is overbearing and dictatorial, but can be survived if flattered sufficiently. Remember these people would rather you stood around praising them than actually did any work. It follows that Leo bosses are quite good about giving parties and gifts, and as long as you agree with everything they say you could be all right. The danger comes when they embark on absurd megalomaniac schemes, which inevitably you will have to carry out. Forming a human pyramid as an advertising stunt may seem like a great idea to your Leo boss, but not such a good plan to you when you're nominated as the person to go on top. The typical profile of a Leo employer is that of a rich fat bully. You're going to have to learn to live with it.

THE LEO EMPLOYEE

There is almost no point in employing a Leo. He or she will inevitably think they know it all, disregard others and spend the day showing off instead of working. They send the rest of the workforce mad with their incessant arrogance and they drive away your customers. On a darker note, remember that the Leo you employ wants your job, and may stop at nothing to get it. If you are a Virgoan, or Piscean or Aquarian, chances are that he has already got it.

YOUR SUN-CYCLE DIARY: LEO – JULY 24th–AUGUST 23rd

July 25th
Perhaps the happiest day of your life: your lucky number comes up in the Golden Jacuzzi Competition and you win a bathful of caviar, appearing on national TV to accept the prize from a glamorous film star.

July 26th
A difficult day spent with the police making an inventory of things stolen from your house while you were at the hoax prize-giving. You still can't believe their theory that you have been set up by someone who 'knows you – and hates you – very thoroughly indeed'.

August 4th

Never one to bear a grudge, you invite all your friends to a party in your somewhat denuded house. You perform several of your legendary party pieces including your rendition of 'My Way' on the little stage beside the bar in the sitting room. Afterwards you find yourself getting along quite famously with a junior colleague from work whom you have always fancied.

August 5th

On waking up, you recognize that last night's conquest is wearing several items of gold personal jewellery stolen in the burglary of a few days ago. You feel hurt, betrayed, sickened, but most of all, anxious to know what this new friend thought of your 'My Way'.

August 6th

Still weighing up the implications of yesterday's violent argument. Is it really possible your junior colleague could have bought the jewellery, along with your floating wax TV lamp, your hi-fi, your record collection and your Colt 45 cigarette lighter, from a classified advertisement in the evening paper?

August 7th

To the library for last week's newspapers. This is what you read: 'Must sell. Contents of entire house to be disposed of soonest. Very cheap.' Only on the way home do you recognize the accompanying telephone number as being your own mother's!

August 10th

After a row like that it looks as if you've lost a mother. But at least your junior colleague was telling the truth, so perhaps you've gained a lover.

August 13th
You've also gained a sense that you're not quite well.

August 14th
Anniversary of the outbreak of WW I. This interesting information, and much else besides, gleaned from long outdated magazines in the waiting room of the Clap Clinic. The doctor prescribes a course of penicillin.

August 20th
Your boss invites you to a champagne reception to celebrate his divorce. Unfortunately, because of the penicillin, you are unable to drink. Your boss interprets this as insubordination.

August 22nd
Your junior colleague is promoted to your job.

August 23rd
Your former boss announces his engagement to your mother.

August 24th
Tests prove you are fatally allergic to penicillin.

KLEENEX
KLEEN
DISINF
VIRGO
VIRGO
VIRGO
VIRGO
VIRGO

VIRGO

August 24th–September 23rd

'The miserable creatures as clean as a whistle
– and as tuneless'

Samuel Johnson

Virgoans are calm, gentle and peace-loving people. They are rather self-contained yet pleasingly exact individuals with a perceptive eye on the world. The Virgo ruling planet is Mercury and their element is Earth – in astrological terms an attractive combination that is certain to produce a rare thoughtful human being, with a five-figure IQ rating. As if all of these qualities weren't enough, Virgoans have a natural gift for friendship.

The information in the foregoing paragraph is a myth – a myth that has been handed down over the aeons by amateur astrologers who should have done their homework better. People who come into contact with Virgoans discover very quickly they qualify for the three 'hyps': hypocritical, hypercritical, and hypochondriacal. They are famous for taking pleasure in making other people feel small (this is rich coming from Virgoans who are renowned for their diminutive size). Dedicated to being seriously obnoxious from a very early age, Virgoans are Numero Uno contenders for the coveted 'Most Unpopular Sign in the Galaxy Award'.

No serious astrologer has yet got a fix on the exact

planetary position which forged the peculiar Virgo character, but it is generally agreed that Mars and Uranus conspired together at the Virgoan birth. Their conspiracy produced some pretty unwholesome characteristics, to say the least. Their hypochrondriacal nature makes them obsessive about personal cleanliness – it's no surprise to learn that the bidet was invented by a Venetian Virgoan in the sixteenth century.

Not only are they obsessed by their own cleanliness, they are also obsessed by the need to survive World War III. A national survey recently revealed that a very high percentage of Virgoans own or are currently building nuclear fall-out shelters. Laugh now, they say, but don't come running to my shelter when the three-minute warning sounds. Contemplating a post-nuclear Virgo world where the Swiss nation (who are all Virgoans) survives in toto, plus an international assortment of fashion designers, hairdressers, dentists and weirdos, persuades the rest of us it wouldn't be worth surviving anyway.

THE VIRGO MAN

The sarcastic ticket collector, the parking attendant, the officious tour guide, and the bossy little man who shouts at everyone to stand back before igniting the firework display, are all Virgo males.

There is a strong possibility that your local hairdresser is a Virgoan and there has to be a likelihood that he is as camp as a row of tents. Add it up. As he rummages around in your mouth your dentist might well mutter something about being a Mercury/Earth person. You work in an office – each time you go to the lavatory you keep seeing that peculiar person from Accounts – yes, he's a Virgo male obsessed with his bodily functions and capable of washing his hands more than ten times every day.

One of the most infamous Virgoans was Pontius Pilate – a man who was only too happy to wash his hands. Contemporary historians tell of Pilate's intense vanity, his highly polished leather sandals and the little compact kit he invariably carried around with him. Pilate set a trend for Virgoans.

THE VIRGO WOMAN

The Sixth female House of Mercury holds many surprises for the astrologically unaware. The Virgo feminine elements are both mutable and negative – a sharp and peppery combination. The Virgo woman is intensely pleased with herself, and intensely displeased with everyone else. She is self-obsessed but lacks the ability to be self-critical. She can reveal a sharp tongue if she wants, and is a little too fond of reducing Piscean and Libran admirers to tears.

Men who settle down with Virgo women realize quite rapidly that they have made a dreadful error in their choice of partner. Virgo females practically invented the art of nagging; they cannot live within a hundred feet of a speck of dirt and will demand that the house be cleaned again and again until it is spotless. Virgo women whisk ashtrays away for cleaning immediately after a little ash has been deposited in them, and are to be seen meticulously rearranging magazines into neat piles, reading newspapers with gloves on (so they don't get printing ink on their hands) and scouring the rims of lavatories with acid.

The bossy sister at the hospital is probably a Virgoan,

as is the hard ambitious career woman. So is the policewoman with thin lips.

VIRGO SEX

Men

A Virgoan's natural or unnatural desires are going to be tempered by the medical implications of a close physical union with another person. Virgoans are paranoid about contracting diseases, and will go to elaborate lengths to check out their prospective partner's medical status. So beware of the man who has been eyeing you at a party and later sidles up and asks you for a blood sample: you've got a Virgo admirer who's hedging his bets.

Assuming your friend is satisfied with your thoroughgoing cleanliness you're in business. But is it the kind of business you like? Virgoans often make love wearing surgeons' green overalls and rubber gloves. They might well insist on brushing their partner's teeth and gargling before kissing. Very romantic. A Leo woman, interviewed by Kinsey in 1948, related the traumatic effect of being actually hoovered down by her Virgo man before having sex. Virgo men often have fantasies about meeting nurses in clinics.

Women

It's just nag-nag-nag with a Virgo woman in bed and out of it. The luckless lover is left wondering what *can* he do right? Virgo women are extremely critical of their partners' performance, and will express dissatisfaction instantly if so inclined. In fact the Virgo-woman experience is a confusing one because she is likely to be making love and attempting to change the sheets at the same time.

As with all cardinally orientated Water signs Virgo women will be disposed to making love near or actually in water. If you're unlucky – and let's face it, you are if you've ended up with a Virgo woman – you could be looking into her eyes with a backdrop of the English Channel. It's November.

THE VIRGO DRIVER

The Virgo driver is a finicky beast who is inclined to do everything according to the Highway Code. Other motorists realize that this actually makes the Virgo driver extremely dangerous, because the obsession with detail can override concentrating on major hazards ahead.

Naturally the Virgo car owner is going to be pretty keen on keeping the vehicle spotlessly clean. It follows then that car washes are virtually kept solvent by Virgo clients as are the companies who make in-car air fresheners. You'll know where to find your Virgo aquaintance on a Sunday morning: outside the semi cleaning the motor. It could be polishing the hubcaps, it could be scouring the ashtrays. In really extreme cases, and we are talking about a diurnal-phase influence here, they have been known to actually vacuum the chassis.

LET'S DRESS VIRGO

Men

In one of Sketchley's more penetrating market surveys it was discovered that a staggering 48 per cent of their male clients were Virgoans! Of these, most were content to have all their clothes dry cleaned on a weekly basis – including socks and underpants – and a really hardline faction representing 2.5 per cent regularly requested that Sketchley's dry clean their shoes.

Just as you'll never catch a Virgo man in a launderette (because of its germ potential), you'll never find him looking as if he didn't step straight out of the dry cleaners (sometimes Virgoans can be spotted shrouded in dry cleaners' polythene for extra protection). This man loves creases and looks at unpressed shirts with horror.

Howard Hughes – a supreme example of the Virgo man – actually wore Kleenex boxes for shoes, so paranoid was he about infection.

Women

Virgo women are as obsessive as their male counterparts when it comes to neatness and personal cleanliness.

The Virgo female wages constant war on body odours. She will buy industrial-size canisters of deodorant spray which are lavishly applied to all parts of the anatomy. Neither can she stand the sight of body hair: Virgo armpits and legs are no stranger to the razor.

Her make-up is applied exactly – with lipstick precisely outlining those traditionally famous thin Virgo lips. Many Virgo women are mistaken for doctors due to their love of white overcoats.

MY FAVOURITE THINGS: VIRGO

Rubber gloves, Howard Hughes, Machiavelli, Debrett's Book of Etiquette, Ivan Lendl, thin ties, Ayatollah

Khomeini, Jerry Falwell, scouring pads, Torvill 'n' Dean, Paul Getty, hypodermic syringes, dry cleaners, Emperor Hirohito, *Pravda*, Dr Kildare, Mr Teasy Weasy, dust-free rooms, garbage disposal, bidets, Bernard Montgomery, Joan Crawford, *The Guardian*, Martina Navratilova, *Salieri*, Eva Peron, Dettol, Mike Read.

YOUR GUIDE TO LOVE: VIRGO

Virgo–Aries
You love telling other people off, and there are opportunities for you aplenty in this Mars/Mercury matching. Your childish Aries partner will need to be scolded and spanked a great deal. You are only too happy to oblige.

Virgo–Taurus
Many people have remarked on the Virgo total lack of humour, and that's one quality you're really going to need if you decide to plump for a Taurean mate. You are rather horrible, while your Taurean partner is incredibly boring. There are any number of negative intergalactic problems here.

Virgo–Gemini
This is a Mercury/Mercury pairing that on the face of it seems to have a lot going for it. However, your suspicious nature is quickly going to focus attention on your devious partner as you will notice that a great number of your most treasured possessions have disappeared.

Virgo–Cancer
You are both cowards, but there the similarity ends. A Virgoan is not exactly an *emotional* person, so it follows

that you are peculiarly unprepared to deal with the frequent ravings and screechings of your Cancer partner. The ruling planet combination of Mercury/Moon only serves to emphasize this appallingly unfortunate pairing.

Virgo–Leo
A Leo likes to explode in a frenzy of self-congratulation and narcissism, and in many ways you're rather pleased with yourself as well – so this relationship has obvious problems in the ego department. A Leo won't take kindly to nagging and criticism, neither will a Leo take pity on you when you claim to be ill – which you do 90 per cent of the time.

Virgo–Virgo
At last somebody who understands all of your faults only too well. It's rather comforting to be with someone who knows all about how fantastically hypercritical, hypocritical and hypochondriacal you really can be.

Virgo–Libra
This is a Mercury/Venus match and one where Venus-Libra gets the roughest deal. Librans are so irritatingly pliable, such turncoats and such ditherers that you really can't resist laying into them with your sharp little tongue. This will be a desperate relationship.

Virgo–Scorpio
You always thought you would have the last word until you met a Scorpio. This strange, powerful, bizarre personality from Mars/Pluto always has to win. You're just rather odd and peculiar when the chips are down, so you're going to lose out here.

Virgo–Sagittarius
Your obsession with order and neatness is going to be severely tested by this clumsy hoofer from the ruling planet of Jupiter. This is the person who juggles with your Dresden china and tramples over your immaculate bonsai trees. It's not as if Sagittarians make up for this gross behaviour by being charming company – in fact they are just plain stupid.

Virgo–Capricorn
Capricorns, like oil in water, rise or attempt to rise in the world. They expect an ingratiating social smarminess from their partners to help them on their way. You have never been able to master easy social familiarity, as a result of which your Capricorn partner will soon be casting around for another mate.

Virgo–Aquarius
A huge vat of lentil wine bubbling over in your spick and span kitchen, three tons of *'Nuclear Power? No Thanks'* stickers boxed-up in the spare room, and yoghourt consommé are not your idea of fun. Think very seriously before committing yourself to an Aquarian partner.

Virgo–Pisces
At last your sharp, peppery and critical nature has one slavish admirer: a Piscean. You can stamp all over your Pisces partner in your neat little shoes. The Jupiter/Neptune person will be wildly applauding your every insult, so grateful is the Piscean for company.

VIRGO FOOD AND ENTERTAINING

This is not a convivial sign, so Virgoans do not enjoy, and rarely give, parties. When they do they are invariably sombre affairs, with the Virgo host or hostess making the guests feel as uncomfortable as possible. Look forward to conversation flowing like glue at a Virgo party.

Virgoans are likely to be on some type of diet and are unwilling to change to reasonable food for one evening's entertaining. So accept a Virgo invitation to dinner at your own risk, and expect the following gastronomic delights:

Starter:
Diced carrot

Main Course:
Scandacrisp soufflé

Pudding:
Brûlée sans crème

Cheese
Scandacrisp and skimmed-milk cheese

Beverage:
Perrier water

VIRGO ON HOLIDAY

The ideal Virgo holiday is to take a two-week break at a health spa, where they can absorb themselves totally in their physical wellbeing. Everybody loves a hypo at a health spa, particularly at £200 a day.

Unable to buy seclusion, poorer Virgoans have a hard time of it on packages and coach tours. Fellow holidaymakers decide quickly that the peculiar, critical Mercury person is someone to be excluded from all events and activities if at all possible.

THE VIRGO EMPLOYER

Remember when your mother would make you take off your shoes before you could come into the house? And brush your teeth after every meal, clean your finger-nails and comb your hair? It's ten times worse working for a Virgo. You can only speak to your employer via sterilized telephone. You can only breathe in. You do get a private health scheme and payment in Swiss francs, but you're not allowed into your own office without first walking through a car-wash and sheep-dip installed in the corridor. Unless you're a Virgoan yourself, take evasive action.

THE VIRGO EMPLOYEE

You need to be either a Virgo or crazy or both (a common enough complaint) to take on a Virgo employee. You thought you were hiring a joker when this character turned up for the interview in a gas-mask, but sadly, that was for real. No one can work with a Virgo, for the simple reason that a Virgo can work with no one else. Cancel the contract of employ-ment if you can, before the entire shop-floor is turned into an operating theatre.

YOUR SUN-CYCLE DIARY: VIRGO – AUGUST 24th–SEPTEMBER 23rd

August 24th
With Neptune, Mercury and Venus all being swept

across the galaxy towards a direct confrontation with Mars, you feel a ghastly foreboding.

August 25th
Having spent all night racked by a sense of atomic doom you decide to invest in your ultimate dream possession – a 'Staysure Multi-Purpose Fall-out Shelter Kit'. A phone call to the company and the swift despatch of a cheque tie the matter up for you.

August 26th
Uranus and Venus are now locked into your astral plane. You're feeling rather smug these days, contemplating the insurance policy you've wisely invested in.

August 31st
An enormous lorry arrives bearing the shelter in various sections. Groaning with effort six men carry the lead-lined parts into your back garden (they were a little upset when you insisted on them removing their boots in order to protect your carpets). With the various sections finally stacked up and gradually sinking into your back-garden turf, the wiseacre foreman gives you the instruction sheets and the men depart. You are particularly glad to see that the instructions inform you that the shelter is good at any distance beyond 200 miles of an atomic explosion – or you get your money back! You live 300 miles away from any viable target, so you allow yourself the sickening smile of a born survivor.

September 9th
Mercury is literally dancing for joy, in your astral plane these days. You've made no secret to your neighbours

of your valuable new possession which even now is taking shape in your back garden.

September 11th
With the shelter erected and kitted out with a huge amount of canned foodstuffs, air fresheners and a king's ransom of pharmaceutical goods, you decide to throw open the doors of your house so your neighbours can see how lucky you are.

September 13th
Beware of some malignant planetary surprises in store.

September 14th
The large sign outside your house 'Come and Inspect a One-Man Nuclear Shelter' fails to attract a single visitor.

September 15th
You are still wondering why no one has visited your shelter until you read the front-page article of your local newspaper: 'Largest UK Cruise Missile Base to be Built Locally'. With a sense of outrage you realize that the perimeter wire will back on to your shelter and your chances of survival within 100 miles – let alone yards – of this prime target will be less than zero.

NOTICE
ME
HOW TO SUPPORT THE GREENHAM COMMON WOMEN
HOW TO LOVE THE BOMB
A
DAS KAPITAL
R
MEIN KAMPF
B
HEALTH FOOD
I
CREAM CAKES
L

LIBRA

September 24th–October 23rd

> 'See how the scales do tip this way and that, so to please the viewer'
>
> *Oliver Goldsmith*

Librans will earnestly tell you that the Sign of the Scales is the most intelligent and gentle Sign in the constellation, and when it comes to sheer niceness – well there just aren't any other contenders in the ring. One of the really lovely things about Librans is that they tell everybody about how fabulously wonderful and popular they are. 'I'm a person person,' they'll say, beaming at a room full of people hurrying for the exit. If Librans do confess to one little fault it's taking time mulling over decisions, but they will defend this by claiming that they're only being true to the Sign of the Scales in carefully weighing up the pros and cons of everyday life.

Libras have a tendency to exaggerate and they certainly exaggerate their worth in other people's eyes. In fact, most people recall them as rather pathetic characters who are pathologically incapable of making any quick decision. It has to be said that even the most mundane things present awful decision-making problems for your average Libran – like deciding which side of the bed to get out of in the morning. Equally it should be stated that some Librans, who were born on the cusp of Uranus, can be as stubborn as mules when they do finally manage to make a decision, and will not alter course lightly.

Another characteristic that Librans are not too keen to talk about, but everyone else is, is their parasitical nature. Librans have an absolutely undoubted ability to lie to, and flatter, those in more powerful positions than themselves (i.e. an awful lot of people). It's a well-known fact that a high percentage of Louis XIV's courtiers were Librans, as were all of Richard Nixon's various spokesmen during the Watergate affair.

It is the devastating Venus/Air combination which produces a trait in the Libran nature that they will never confess to, but which all serious astrologers know to be true: you can find a strong trace of the opposite sex in them. While in few cases being actually hermaphrodite, a great number of Librans have real difficulty in deciding which sex they are.

Despite their occasional surface gloss, in their heart of hearts Librans know that they run through the race of life with their shoelaces tied together. If they don't succeed in ingratiating themselves with people they wish to impress they can become sulky and quarrelsome. Born at a time of year when winter is fast approaching, the triurnal modes are all wrong for this unlucky Sign.

THE LIBRA MAN

The Libra man is anxious to be accepted in the world. Allied to this intense desire for acceptance and popularity is the legendary Libran gullibility. Naturally this makes him a superb target for those people who have dedicated their lives to exploiting others – Capricorns and Geminis spring to mind. Many's the time a Libra male has been persuaded into 'coming up with the cash' for a large stake in a company which designs square car tyres, or been talked into investing in a project to manufacture diesel-powered toasters. One Libra man from Idaho was recently parted from a lifetime's savings for a major stake in McDonald's planned expansion into the Iranian market.

Ripped off, insulted and laughed at, the Libra male just won't give up on his quest for global popularity. The cocky little bloke in the pub who says 'cheers' and 'to see you, nice' to total strangers is virtually certain to be a Libran – he makes spurious bonhomie a way of life. It follows that the greasy theatrical agent or press attaché, the company spokesman, and the man in the shiny suit with more dandruff to play with than is good for him are also Libra men. Nice one, Scales man, we love you.

THE LIBRA WOMAN

Dominated as she is by the feminine element of Air and propelled through life by the force of Venus, it's natural to conclude that the Libra woman is going to be weighed on the Scales of Love for the duration of her life. Reared on the conviction that she is incredibly attractive to the opposite sex, the Libra female enters maturity with her heart full of Mills and Boon scenarios and concentrating on the wonderful world of men. The real world of overweight balding males who haven't seen their feet in years, eat cheese and onion crisps, fart first thing in the morning, and who are likely to be indifferent after the first close encounter comes as a traumatic shock to her.

It is this first grapple with the realities of life that makes the Libra woman so determined not only to be noticed for her body – such as it is – but also her mind. The Seventh female House of the Zodiac is the pre-eminent feminine Sign which says 'notice me'. In order to be noticed she will not only wear dangerously outlandish clothes, but will develop a very strident line in argument and debate. Unfortunately she is likely to be extremely contradictory. The lady at the party shouting for the spotlight to hit her, whilst loudly defending the nuclear arms race and seconds later proclaiming sisterhood with the Greenham Common women is certainly a Libra woman. You'll know who to avoid that evening, if you know what's good for you.

On the housekeeping front the Libra female has a dreadful reputation. She is certain to exceed the monthly budget handsomely and her lack of responsibility ensures that she sweeps the dust under the carpet both literally and metaphorically.

LIBRA SEX

Men

The introduction to the Libra character clearly warned that there is a strong trace of the opposite sex to be found in these people – particularly amongst so-called Libra 'males'. Any woman contemplating a relationship with a Libra 'man' would be well advised to check whether her prospective little chum is in fact male. He might not be. He might be a woman, or even more confusingly both male and female. However it must be said that the majority of Libra males are – surprisingly

– actually of the male gender, though more than capable of greatly exaggerating their attractiveness to the opposite sex.

The art of seduction must involve a series of fairly straightforward decisions, so it follows that Libra men are pretty handicapped when it comes to this department. Many prospective partners have been somewhat disappointed by the Libran's panicky habit of turning off the lights in the restaurant in which they are dining and completely removing his clothes – these things are supposed to happen later, if at all. The classic Libran male's situation is not being able to decide exactly the right moment to put his arm round the girl. He'll probably count up to his lucky number, and having reached it decide to count sheep. There's always a reason for postponement in the Libran's world. Though he pretends to be full of bluster and sexual savoir faire, when it comes down to it he thinks that the Kama Sutra is an Indian restaurant. Those women who have gone further with Libra men than a visit to the local cinema have been annoyed by their habit of nervously waving to them in bed.

Women

A Libra woman will go to unusual lengths to attract the opposite sex, so much so that she throws all caution to the winds, often ending up in dangerous and sexually compromising situations. As her Capricorn or Scorpio partner is helping her into the rubber gladiator's uniform she might well have second thoughts about gladly accepting the invitation to the Toga Party. Later, as she is subjected to a series of athletic, complicated and painful movements involving a trident and a net she'll have third and even fourth thoughts – but it'll be too late.

The unavoidable truth is that the Eighth and Thirteenth Houses of Venus boldly associate Libran woman with the world of love. However, she simply lacks the savvy to survive unexploited for long in the sexual jungle. As one particularly ruthless Scorpio remarked 'This lady isn't street – or sheet – wise.'

She's sociable, more than a little gullible and pathetically eager to please, so consequently an open season has been declared on Libra women.

THE LIBRA DRIVER

It is a well-known fact that Librans find driving cars extremely difficult. Driving requires a series of fairly elementary decisions like when to brake, to put the headlights on at night, and to actually utilize the windscreen wipers when it's raining. A Libra driver can be in the ugly situation of hurtling towards traffic lights at 70 mph and still be weighing up the pros and cons of braking. No prizes for guessing that these people make for extremely dangerous and uncoordinated drivers.

The British School of Motoring test survey of 1981 more than bore out this argument when they discovered that more Librans failed their tests than any other Sign. They were generally failed very quickly because they could not decide: (a) which car door to open; (b) which key to put in the ignition; (c) whether to turn the wheel when going round a corner.

It's comparatively easy to spot those few Librans who make it on to the road without L-plates, because they love waving at passing motorists. The sticker on their rear window reads something encouraging like 'I'm a

Libran – get close to me' or 'Please help me drive this car'. What an irritating Sign this is.

LET'S DRESS LIBRA

Men

If there's a Libra man around you could well be looking at an ID bracelet which bears the legend 'Vince', or it might be two-tone shoes and a pair of absurdly generous jacket lapels. At a very extreme level, involving any number of astral complexities at the nativity, you could be staring in utter amazement at a man wearing zebra-skin swimming trunks. Libra men are more than capable of wearing 'I Love New York' T-shirts even though they've never set foot in the New World.

Women

The Libra woman has more or less similar tastes to those of her male counterpart when it comes to clothes. She loves to be noticed, indeed absolutely *has* to be noticed – so will go to extreme lengths to obtain the 'rave reviews' she craves. It's no surprise to learn that fishnet stockings and the mini-skirt were both invented by Libra women. A Libra woman from Sydney was the first person to win a lucrative prize established by an eccentric millionaire: to keep 3 lb of make-up on her face for more than 24 hours, whilst running up and down.

Most Libra women have face-lifts when they get older. With a good handful of flesh pinned behind their ears their faces take on a distinctly oriental appearance. Rich Libra women adore carting around chihuahuas which they like to dress up.

MY FAVOURITE THINGS: LIBRA

Arthur Scargill, James Boswell, autograph books, Margaret Thatcher, Lionel Blair, Dick van Dyke, Habitat, Jerry Williams, Duran Duran, Michael Heseltine, Julio Iglesias, Demis Roussos, Hofmeister lager, Boy George, Gary Hart, David Frost, Pineapple Dance Studios, brush cuts, Danny la Rue, Nike shoes, Brigham Young, Golf GTIs, Nik Kershaw, Oscar Wilde, Gloria Hunniford.

YOUR GUIDE TO LOVE: LIBRA

Libra–Aries
If you serve trifle and promise to have a conjuror this is someone who will come to all of your parties, and given the number of refusals you get, that can't be bad. Aries people think that you, and everyone else, are terribly grown-up. The Venus/Mars astral combination only serves to underline the superb prospects for this relationship.

Libra–Taurus
Taureans are not only fatuous but desperately boring people. You are both capable of being stubborn given the right circumstances, so there may well be dreadful arguments and fights to look forward to in this relationship. You might have to get used to your Taurean partner throwing copies of the *Daily Telegraph* at you, while your Taurus friend is going to have to acclimatize to you shaking dandruff everywhere as you go into one of your rages. In truth, the answer to the potential of this relationship is written in the stars: you are Venus/Air, while Taurus is Venus/Earth – a cosmic cul-de-sac.

Libra–Gemini
With their criminal minds, Geminians are going to take you for everything you've got. They seem so nice at first, so interested in you as a deeply wonderful person, it's only when you notice your savings have been transferred to a numbered account in the Cayman Islands that you begin to get a little worried.

Libra–Cancer
You're not absolutely decided about your Cancer partner, and for once in your life your indecisiveness is justified. Cancerians are totally emotional people – one minute up, the next minute shrieking out their displeasure at some imagined wrong. You simply have to accept that people are going to like you even less than normal if you've got a Cancer partner in tow.

Libra–Leo
Librans and Leos have in common an insatiable quest for popularity, but you are going to be severely tested by your Leo partner's quite extraordinary egoism. Your cry of 'Notice Me' is going to be drowned out by the leonine roar of 'I, Me, Mine'.

Libra–Virgo
Virgoans are strange fastidious people given to obsessional habits. You're rather a simplistic person in many ways, who is going to find it difficult living with a person who dresses in Clingfilm to avoid contact with germs.

Libra–Libra
You understand each other, up to a point. But Librans are capable of denying their worst traits so you'll both attempt – a little pathetically – to come on really strong

on the decision front. It has to be said that this relationship is not a wholly relaxing proposition.

Libra–Scorpio
It will take little effort for your Scorpio partner to whip you into line for some minor domestic misdemeanour – the simple removal of one of your fingernails should do the trick – so you should be particularly careful to do everything correctly and above all don't get sulky and quarrelsome. Even you, with your boundless enthusiasm, can't admit to enjoy being tortured.

Libra–Sagittarius
The sheer stupidity of your Sagittarian partner will at first astonish then delight you, as you realize your gap-toothed friend is wildly applauding your every move.

Libra–Capricorn
You'll enjoy being around a Capricorn and likely as not going up through society on the back of your social-climbing Goat. Capricorns love having you around as well, because of your gift for flattering those people whom they also wish to impress. Very good prospects here.

Libra–Aquarius
After getting hitched to an Aquarian, life can take on the complexity of a bad trip. Your freaky friend is up to any number of unsociable tricks which are going to really upset you, like experimenting with scary drugs, making love potions from nettles and associating with major left-wing terrorist groups. You're in for a fab time, Libra.

Libra–Pisces
A Venus/Jupiter/Neptune triune. This sounds astrologically impressive until you realize that you've settled down with somebody who scarcely qualifies for the description 'human being' – the use of which term would suggest that Pisceans possess sparks of humanity, which is wholly untrue.

LIBRA FOOD AND ENTERTAINING

With one eye on the popularity stakes, Scales people frequently entertain. For both poor and rich Librans, giving parties on a modest or lavish budget is an essential must.

However, their usual indecisiveness is strongly in evidence as far as cooking is concerned. Most Libra cooks are very uncertain about what to put into a meal, so they are likely to be running around like headless chickens seconds before the guests arrive, and are liable to have panicked and thrown a whole variety of ingredients into a dish in record time. Here is the likely Libra food experience. Take out life insurance now, if you're dining chez Libra.

Starter:
Onion soup – or was it carrot? Well, a bit of both actually; sorry about the blancmange.

Main Course:
Duck à chicken. Anyway, some type of bird. Sorry about the feathers.

Pudding:
Chocolate mousse. Couldn't find any chocolate, but hope you like it anyway.

Beverage:
Anything you like really – couldn't decide on what wine, so here's a pint of Bailey's.

LIBRA ON HOLIDAY

Librans are the travel agent's dream customers. They are certain to postone the decision on when to take their holiday until the last minute, allowing the agent to step in and boldly sell the gullible Libran packages nobody else wants. The Libran holiday might well be spent sightseeing in Lagos or waterskiing round Iceland in November, but most probably it will be spent in a Spanish hotel with medieval sanitary facilities and 'quick access to local transport systems' (the more wily traveller will know that this means the hotel actually sits on the central reservation of a motorway). Always the cocky enthusiast, the Libran will report on the hotel as being 'fabulous'.

With the Mars/Venus axis tilting away from the diurnal equinox (as it is likely to do during the summer months), the Libran on holiday is more keen than ever to be accepted by fellow holidaymakers. This is the person who lends you suntan oil, buys endless rounds of drinks – even gives you money – and later asks what you and your group of friends are doing that evening. Avoiding the Libran, that's what they're doing.

THE LIBRA EMPLOYER

Very few Librans make it to the level where they actually employ people. Those that do are unlikely to hold down their jobs for long. Obviously their inability to make quick decisions is a tremendous handicap in the world of business. A Libra 'Executive' (i.e. decision-maker) is a total contradiction in terms.

THE LIBRA EMPLOYEE

With their surface charm, some Librans can actually fool an interviewer who is lacking in perception and intelligence – for instance Sagittarians or Taureans – into employing them. Very soon, the latent Libran irresponsibility comes to the fore. It might take the form of telling a rival organization all the firm's most jealously guarded secrets, or pledging the entire company profits to someone who's been nice to them, or it could just be simply throwing away all incoming mail without reading it. If you've been stupid enough to employ this person, you deserve everything that's coming to you.

YOUR SUN-CYCLE DIARY: LIBRA – SEPTEMBER 24th–OCTOBER 23rd

September 24th
This is your month and you just know that everyone is going to love and admire you for the truly wonderful person you really are. You have resolved to get a grip on your indecisiveness, and bearing this in mind it only takes you fifteen minutes to decide which side of the bed to get out of, and – a record for you – three minutes to put your left foot into your left shoe and a further two minutes to decide which foot to put the other one on.

September 27th
With Saturn and Uranus drifting seductively into your niche in the galaxy, you rightly conclude it's a propitious time for developing your love life. Be warned, however, that you should not believe everything that you hear in the coming days.

September 29th
Saturn and Uranus play host to a surprise guest: Venus. Now you've really come up trumps on the romantic front!

October 1st
An Aries aquaintance contacts you. Someone has dropped out of the party planned for tomorrow, would you like to come? Of course you would, you little go-getter!

October 2nd
At the party you introduce yourself at least twice to all of the other guests. Later you are seated next to an extremely attractive member of the opposite sex. After a while the conversation drifts to vacations – it seems your glamorous companion is a big wheel in the travel business. This marvellous person knows of some superb round-the-world cruises which are unbelievably good value. Would you be interested? You eagerly arrange to meet soon to purchase a cruise ticket, and while you're about it, to pursue the amorous potential of this lucky encounter.

October 6th
Saturn and Uranus are still controlling your destiny with an almighty tight rein, but – a note of warning – Venus has disappeared as fast as she arrived.

October 10th
A freak diurnal equinox promises fairly seismic shocks for you in the near future, unless you show extreme caution.

October 13th
The day of your reunion with your attractive travel-agent friend. After dinner at a discreet restaurant this person accepts your outrageously daring invitation to come back to your place for a 'cup of coffee'.

October 14th
You still can't believe what happened last night. Your erstwhile friend persuaded you to pay £1,500 cash up front for the cruise ticket, and gave you an address where to pick it up. Having got that out of the way your subsequent amorous advances were fiercely resisted, and your attractive friend left muttering something about dandruff. Still you've gained an unbelievably good value holiday, even if you've lost a potential lover.

October 17th
Buoyed up with enthusiasm and visions of palm-fringed beaches you are finally able to get away to collect the ticket from the given address only to find, with a mounting sense of hysteria, that it doesn't actually exist.

SCORPIO

SCORPIO
October 24th–November 22nd

'At the tail, a merciless venom'

Orestes

Scorpios get respect from their fellow men. That respect is based on the legendary Scorpio loyalty, their calmness, tolerance, and ability to put people at their ease (the symbolic bright star of Antares dominates this Sign). Scorpio has nine spiritual fires, each of them making its own contribution to the amazing Scorpio character. If there has been a confluence of Aquarius, Gemini and Leo in the nativity, then that Scorpio is indeed *highly* special. Scorpios born with that celestial combination – and there are quite a few of them believe it or not – are incredibly special people.

Scorpios will enjoy reading the foregoing paragraph. The natural arrogance and selfishness that is theirs will take that description as read. Others have come to know better about 'this highly evolved specimen'. Many will agree that the most notable characteristic of Scorpio people is their amazing cruelty, their indifference, their cheerful enjoyment at the wilful destruction of all who stand in their way. The need to cause pain to others starts young. Many people will recall the little Scorpio boy in the playground at school hunched over some wingless fly, or the Scorpio girl who was fond of sticking pins into voodoo dolls and models of the biology teacher. These activities are harmless when compared to those practised by the adult Scorpio – where calculated violence to other human beings rather than insects is the keynote, and the pins are exchanged for more sophisticated tools of torture.

Scorpios crave power as a natural springboard for indulging their strange tastes. Ideally this means being the head of a vast international conglomerate, with daily opportunities for kicking the hell out of those junior to them. However – power being a popular commodity – it may not always be possible for them to operate from these exalted levels. Though a strong word of warning is necessary: do not underestimate the spite and nuisance value of the average Scorpio, be he or she bank clerk, traffic warden, third world diplomat or mercenary (particularly the latter).

It is a known fact that most Presidents of the United States have been Scorpios, an ideal platform from which to launch vendettas against others. However, it is heartening to dwell on how many of those Presidents have been assassinated during the course of their tenure in office (but sobering when you realize that their assassins were all Scorpios).

Most people are agreed that Scorpios are pretty unsavoury characters and the world would be a better place without them. To this end a small clandestine operation was started thirty-five years ago – Eleven Signs for Eradication of Scorpio: ESEOS. To date the success rate has not been startling, though the tattered remnants of the organization are still in operation and the monthly newsletter *Scorpcontrol* is still issued from a secret address in Horsham.

THE SCORPIO MAN

Having read the introduction to the Scorpio character with rising concern you will be interested in discovering how to recognize Scorpio males quickly and thus avoid them.

Scorpio males tend to be tall, but a few are exceedingly small (there are very few of average height). The small ones usually resemble stick insects dressed in clothes – spindly arms and legs, and large heads with protuberant blue eyes (a common Scorpio feature). A classic Scorpio male of this kind was Josef Goebbels – Hitler's sinister propaganda minister. Do not underestimate small Scorpio men, who can be pretty lethal – particularly in bunkers. They can also be murderously effective in competitive games that favour small people.

At the other end of the spectrum large Scorpio men are rather terrifying. They rarely blink. They have to win at sports. They wear well-cut suits. They carry flick-knives. Their shoes are always well polished. They are great schemers. They are people to avoid at all costs.

THE SCORPIO WOMAN

Picture yourself as a Dalmatian puppy (it may be difficult – but try). You like having a skin, but quite unreasonably somebody else wants it. That somebody is Cruella de Ville who typifies the archetypal Scorpio woman.

Whilst recognizing that the Scorpio female is hell on wheels, it has to be admitted that many are physically attractive. But let this be a broadcast alarm to all male readers: you take an enormous risk in dating a Scorpio female. You are likely to wake up from your drugged stupor next morning to discover that a vital piece of your anatomy has disappeared.

SCORPIO SEX

Men

Scorpio men love sex. In that respect they're not too different from the rest of us (except of course Pisceans who never get any). But do not be fooled, oh innocent Aquarian or Libran women, into thinking that just because he loves sex, he's going to love you into the bargain. Nothing could be further from the truth. Pluto males are surprisingly keen – almost fixated – on the more bizarre types of sexual experimentation.

Scorpios delight in preying upon the weaker species who are easily gulled into thinking that their Scorpio man is just another guy who's big on athleticism, until he winds down a pair of pulleys over the bed and produces a pair of mega-voltage jump leads. The only thing you can pray for is a power failure.

Women

A lot of men who go the full fifteen rounds with a Scorpio woman lose their hair, and their confidence. It takes someone as blithely ignorant as a Sagittarian who has no real conception of pain thresholds to contemplate this proposition with eagerness.

Those men who have dated Scorpio women and recovered their abililty to speak, if not their hair, recall an experience that is not unlike running for fifty miles on burning coals whilst being flailed. We really do advise strongly against the Pluto woman experience, unless you're a Sagittarian, in which case go ahead, Horse Man, sling your Bow and Arrow and do battle. May the best man win.

THE SCORPIO DRIVER

Overtake a Scorpio driver at great personal risk. Likely as not the Scorpio vehicle will be equipped with Boadicea type 'tyre slashers'. These people can be very vindictive if they're not treated as absolute masters of the highway. Quite often Scorpios will drive at 50 mph along motorways, causing a huge tailback of Pisceans, Virgoans and Aquarians who are just too terrified to overtake them.

Scorpios are often seen in places like Eastbourne – they like old people who cross roads slowly and can be easily lined up.

LET'S DRESS SCORPIO

Men

Scorpio men favour black – even for their underpants! They go for the hooded black monk's-cowl look, or the ultimate in Scorpio chic: the SAS uniform!

Some Scorpio men will – by day – restrain these impulses, wearing relatively conventional clothes. But don't be fooled – there's a distinct touch of the dandified and cruel rake to Scorpio men and they are unable to resist the temptation to dress up.

Women

Scorpio women will, like their male counterparts, favour black as their primary colour. The femme-fatale look (strictly for those under 10 stone) is generally popular with Scorpio women, i.e. elbow-length gloves, cigarette holders (for non-smokers), gold chains on *both* ankles, and black fedoras. For those over 10 stone and on a sliding scale up to a terrifying 25, the same dress techniques are usually adopted, but are not considered to be sensationally attractive.

MY FAVOURITE THINGS: SCORPIO

Adolf Hitler, Texas Chain Saw Massacre, Marquis de Sade, the Stranglers, General Pinochet, Caligula, Engelbert Humperdinck, Vita Sackville West, thumbscrews, sulphuric acid, video nasties, Sweeney Todd, Henry VIII, Lucretia Borgia, strappado, Josef Stalin, Norman Tebbit, the Spanish Inquisition, Brian Clough, the Hellfire Club, J. R. Ewing.

YOUR GUIDE TO LOVE: SCORPIO

Scorpio–Aries
Your element is Fire and your fixed aspect is Paraquat which will give you no problems in really sorting out the volatile immature Arietan mixture of Fire and Wind. Your Aries partner will frequently misbehave and will have to be sent to bed early and soundly smacked, preferably with a large cricket bat.

Scorpio–Taurus
You're a dynamic thrusting sadist with a bent for physical and mental torture and you've settled down with an old carpet slipper? Forget it.

Scorpio–Gemini

All the ingredients here for a caring, loving relationship with this supercharged Mercury–Mars/Pluto combination. As your Gemini partner languishes in the top security wing of Broadmoor you can show exactly how loving and caring you are by, for instance, sending him/her Christmas cards in August (signed 'with love from both of us').

Scorpio–Cancer

Paraquet/Pepsi makes for a pretty lethal mixture in anyone's book! This could be a surprisingly poisonous relationship, and right up your street.

Scorpio–Leo

Leo's a very selfish sign and vain to boot, so there's plenty of scope here for you to play vicious practical jokes like dressing your Leo partner entirely in gold spandex and taking him/her to a Royal Garden Party!

Scorpio–Virgo

Virgo, deeply influenced by Mercury, is an intensely hypochondriacal sign with a mania for cleanliness. You've got plenty of manias yourself, but keeping your hands clean isn't one of them. This person will irritate you very quickly.

Scorpio–Libra

Librans have a built-in facility for exploitation which is all you're really after in life. This could be an exceptionally happy pairing.

Scorpio–Scorpio

Only your Scorpio partner will know how essentially evil you are and, realizing this early in your relationship, you should level with each other and decide to be deeply unpleasant to others.

Scorpio–Sagittarius
You've got an exceptionally quick and lethal mind, while your Sagittarian partner is an intensely stupid person. A big plus point is: you can get away with absolute murder in this relationship. A big minus point is: Sagittarians present no mental challenges to you whatsoever.

Scorpio–Capricorn
Capricorn's ruling planet is Mercury with the dynamic element of Earth thrown in and the fixed astral aspect of a Triumph TR7. You will find yourself hating your Capricorn partner rather seriously after a while.

Scorpio–Aquarius
This is the dawning of the age of Aquarius! Except it's been dawning for a good few decades now with no visible sign of sunrise. A very incompatible relationship this – a schemer like you getting hitched to a hopeless dreamer.

Scorpio–Pisces
Opportunities are here aplenty for even the average Scorpio to walk roughshod over one of life's natural doormats.

SCORPIO FOOD AND ENTERTAINING

When a Scorpio entertains, don't expect 'Mom's Apple Pie'. In fact don't even count on surviving the meal, as Scorpios often take a perverse pleasure in poisoning their guests. The classic Scorpio dinner party will see guests slumping face down into their eel soup, or staggering across the candlelit room clutching their throats after the genial 'mein host' has handed round a box of After Eights laced with arsenic.

If people dare to come to a Scorpio dinner party they will often bring some tame little taster with them – usually a Piscean, or even better a Taurean – who will eat *anything*.

So prepare yourself for the ultimate Scorpio culinary experience:

First Course:
Dead Sea eel soup (host will boil live eels before astonished guests)

Main Course:
Stuffed Haitian chicken heads aux voodoo

Pudding:
Bombe gâteau

Cheese:
Ethiopian snake cheese

Beverage:
Chianti al Borgia

SCORPIO ON HOLIDAY

Scorpios rarely take time off from advancing their careers. When they *do* take a break there is no creature in the animal kingdom more loathsome and dangerous to be with than the Scorpio 'en vacances' and 'au plage'!

It's always a Scorpio man who will organize the queue at the dodgy Majorcan hotel canteen; who speaks fluent Spanish; who gets away with tipping the taxi driver derisively; who is the only tourist not to be seen wearing sandals – the list is endless.

In short they get off on being considered different from the herd, even on a package holiday. They end up by being disliked by their fellow holidaymakers, but feared as well.

THE SCORPIO EMPLOYER

This person will want to control you and exploit you. You have several options available – none of them easy or attractive:

a) Poison him/her
b) Expose this unremitting sadist to your union
c) Get another job

THE SCORPIO EMPLOYEE

If you are an employer and you have a Scorpio employee simply reverse the above paragraph.

YOUR SUN-CYCLE DIARY: SCORPIO – OCTOBER 24th–NOVEMBER 22nd

October 24th
The first day in your sun cycle. You are entering the time of the triumphant Phoenix. However, there is little triumph in patrolling the streets of London in your Traffic Warden's uniform. You spend the day plastering windscreens with parking tickets and turning spitefully away from imploring, impoverished motorists.

October 25th
The second day in your sun cycle. Last night you had a marvellous dream in which you were personally responsible for wheel-clamping all vehicles in Central London.

October 29th
With Mars on the rampage an exciting day right from the word go, when on a pretext you pick a fight with the milkman. As you leave for work he is experiencing some difficulty in breathing, having a milk bottle lodged in his throat.

November 3rd
A day spent malevolently plotting how you are going to take out the swarthy Libyan diplomat in the grey Mercedes who persistantly disregards your parking tickets.

Novmber 4th
Your pre-breakfast get-fit programme hits an all-time high when you manage to crack *two* walnuts between your buttocks. A strong capacity for creative plotting today as you enter the cyclical equinox.

November 5th
Spotting the familiar Mercedes parked on double yellows by the Habib Bank you immediately make your way to the nearest call box. The switchboard at Scotland Yard quickly routes your call through to the anti-terrorist unit. They immediately see your point about a spectacular fireworks display in Central London, emanating from a Mercedes with Libyan CD plates which is loaded with dynamite. Smirking, you watch with intense satisfaction as the Libyan diplomat is

surrounded by police and hauled off for some unsympathetic questioning while his car is carefully dismantled.

November 9th
Life has been rather dull since the removal of the Libyan.

November 15th
With the cyclical equinox passing through its final stages there is little to look forward to apart from the new edition of *Guns and Ammo* next week.

SAGITTARIUS

SAGITTARIUS

November 23rd–December 21st

'Thy bow is drawn
Thine arrow flieth
Thy foot is wounded'

Johannes Greggins

Look at the Sagittarian, ruled by Jupiter, occupant of the Zodiac's Ninth House. Strong, honest and true. Not delicate, but engagingly direct. Not intellectual, but possessed of a homely wisdom that means more to a friend than all the philosophizing in the world. Warm, affectionately physical, full of stamina and loyalty and fearlessly daring when necessary. Now . . . take off the rose-tinted glasses of myth and imagination and, just for once, face the barely faceable facts. Sagittarians are clumsy, boorish, dense, tactless and totally unacceptable in civilized society. Sagittarius is the sign of the archer, half-human and half-horse. Many people find it hard to tell which half is which.

Sagittarians break things, usually by accident, but sometimes deliberately too. They will smash television sets reflecting unsatisfactory soccer results and rip apart necklaces their clumsy fingers fail to fasten. Sagittarians frequently tread in dog messes. They bump into ornaments, stamp on your toes, stand on your cat, punch you on the shoulder when you're carrying a tray of drinks, they fall off their high heels, they crash their cars into your living room. And they never apologize. Sagittarians like sport. They gain reassurance from team games and boisterous post-match 'larking about'. They like singing on coaches, emptying drinks on to innocent passers-by and accusing other people of being spoil-sports. Ninety-two per cent of Duke of Edinburgh Gold Award winners are Sagittarians and, by the same token, a similar percentage of Boy Scouts and Girl Guides labour beneath the sign of the bow and arrow. For many a Sagittarian, the most intense and artistic experience of a lifetime will occur around the campfire. For others, relaxing in the dorm after a tough game, the poems of Rod McKuen provide a moment of sublime insight into the mysteries of human behaviour.

Sagittarians, who needs 'em?

THE SAGITTARIUS MAN

There is a man on the beach, so covered in black, springy hair that he appears to be wearing a fancy-dress gorilla suit. It is even sprouting from his shoulders. He is shaped like a barrel and parades up and down in a pair of extremely small swimming briefs. A Leo showing off, you might think, but you'd be wrong. There are no gold medallions. This man is not so much showing off as revelling in himself and his unappealing body. The sheer vacancy of his expression, the total stupidity of his behaviour, indicate Sagittarius. This is a man who kicks sand in his own face.

Sagittarian men are not in fact show-offs. In many ways they are lonely people. Their oafing around can hide some complex personality problems. Most Sagittarians are still virgins at thirty. They live alone and sweat a lot. However, they still think of themselves as 'one of the boys'. Every Sagittarian will tell you that he is one of the boys as if this were something to be very proud of, and when he is with the boys, he is indeed quite unmistakable. Forever backslapping and throwing people in the showers after a match (annoying behaviour when your team has just lost, and Sagittarians are some of life's major losers), pretending to be a rally-driver on quiet suburban roads, 'game hunting' with a bow and arrow and machine gun across Africa, or, if pushed, a municipal golf-course, he's a bore. He is coarse and physical and given to drinking too much, then throwing up in Indian restaurants. He is a keen 'survivalist', paying good money to attend ludicrous evening classes given by men who make patently fraudulent claims to have been in the SAS and purporting to show how to catch rabbits and kill off old ladies after 'the big one' has been dropped.

Just occasionally, the Sagittarian chart will be affected by Venus drifting across Jupiter and this will lead to a strange thing: a Sagittarian who is not fond of sports. This truly pathetic man has literally nothing to recommend him.

Sagittarian males of all kinds have big trouble finding the way out of telephone boxes or revolving doors. A startling 80 per cent of WW II Kamikaze pilots are now known to have been Sagittarians. Their commanders told them to fly through the enemy ships on the way home. You couldn't accuse the Sagittarian male of being over-intelligent.

THE SAGITTARIUS WOMAN

The most common kind of Sagittarian female, born with Jupiter at the dead centre of a disappointingly dull

Zodiacal chart, is a walking catastrophe. Walking, what is more, in a pair of heavy-duty rambling boots. The Sagittarian girl is the outdoors type at heart; tweed skirts and combinations are her favoured apparel. She drinks from a hip flask, is very enthusiastic without being in the least bit intelligent, and is usually regarded by her acquaintances as at best a harmless idiot, at worst a tedious nuisance. The hobbies section of her curriculum vitae looks like a syllabus for an Outward Bound course. This Sagittarian is no stranger to canoes. She gets on well with animals – particularly dogs, hawks and horses – but not too well with men. She knows about sex because she has seen the deer rutting on one of her walking holidays, but she does not see what the fuss is about. It looks cold and uncomfortable and she's not going to let anyone fumble around inside her arctic-proof quilted anorak for that kind of fun, thank you very much. The Sagittarian female would prefer to be playing charades at a country house-party, or supervising the difficult midnight birth of a new foal.

When Jupiter slides out of the middle bounds round the edge of the Sagittarian natal frame, dragging the influence of Venus more into effect, a lot of affinity with the great outdoors goes with it. The traditional Sagittarian enthusiasm, of course, coupled with a crass ineptitude in all things, remains, but tends to channel itself into less sporty pursuits, often showbusiness. The ageing hoofer who year in, year out, watches other girls plucked from the chorus line to become stars while she keeps smiling and hopelessly hoping is a typical Sagittarian – the talentless trier. The off-key Shirley Bassey lookalike belting out her numbers in second-rate clubs is another, and a remarkable 85 per cent of conjuror's assistants, sawn in half twice nightly for almost no salary at all, are Sagittarians.

Sagittarian women push the 'pull' door, play golf in the snow – with a white ball – and in truth are best left to their own devices.

SAGITTARIUS SEX

Men

Indeed, for all their macho sportiness and vulgar joking, most Sagittarian men are very shy of women and sex. Some believe that sex before a match will weaken them dangerously, and since there is always another match on the horizon, they never get around to testing out the theory. Others suffer such humiliation at the rejection of their oafish advances at adolescent parties, that they never again dare to venture into the mysterious world of women, preferring to stand in the kitchen drinking from a quart-size can of Ruddles and singing Rugby songs for the rest of their party-going days. The 'survivalist' types amongst Sagittarians do have a somewhat grittier attitude to the fair sex, but no sane woman was ever turned on by a Bowie knife and, like their sporty brothers, these Sagittarians will tend to retreat behind their driving shades and just tell boring stories about what might have been.

Most survivors of sex with Sagittarian men will tell you that driving is not the only thing they do at high speed. They also report feeling as if they have just been through an all-in wrestling match. The Sagittarian, of course, would *rather* have been through an all-in wrestling match – something with rules, a winner and a loser – than struggle to learn this new sport, the point of which is lost to him.

Women

While some mothers do worry about entrusting their daughters to the company of long-striding, tweed-skirted, hearty hockey-playing Sagittarians, it must be said that most of these member of the Zodiac's Ninth House are strictly heterosexual, if they are sexual at all. A lot of Sagittarian women feel that sex is really not very nice, or certainly not as nice as a good long walk with a dog. Your seduction of some Sagittarian women is going to have to feature an elementary biology lesson at some time, but those that have got beyond the gooseberry-bush phase of erotic knowledge generally follow the old Sagittarian principles of grinning and bearing it because the show must go on. Desperately unimaginative and (literally) painfully clumsy but ever willing to join in and do the right thing, the Sagittarian woman can be quite a godsend to the perverted Scorpio who is soon able to convince her of the totally normal practice of electro-convulsive foreplay. For anyone else, however, sex with a Sagittarian woman is going to be one of the most miserable events of a lifetime.

THE SAGITTARIUS DRIVER

When Sagittarians drive, they like to hit more than the road. The ultimate vehicle for them is a four-wheel-drive Cherokee pick-up, sitting fifteen feet off the ground and pulling a small howitzer. But whatever the car, watch out. The Sagittarian's big clumsy feet are forever falling on the wrong pedal, their large ungainly hands are frequently employed on a pocket video-game when at least one should be steering, their eyes are often on the rear-view mirror as they check their hair or make-up – while driving at 70 mph down the motorway. Few Sagittarians smoke – the matches overflowing from the ashtray are the result of trying to light the heater. These people are not bright. Favourite car sticker: 'Designed by a genius, built by a robot, driven by a moron'.

LET'S DRESS SAGITTARIUS

Men

The Sagittarian dressed for his favourite outdoor pursuit of four-wheel drive deerhunting can be a terrifying sight. He looks like an army surplus store on the move, from his shin-high combat boots (with specially concealed Bowie-knife holder) to his two-hundred-pocket survival jacket (spurning the more continental anorak, the Sagittarian prefers to invest in a new centrally heated life-support system specially developed for the Swedish police). When relaxing, he favours inordinately expensive running shoes and football shorts worn outside tracksuit trousers, the ensemble being topped-off by his old school rugby shirt, and a golf pullover with a prominent brand-name symbol on the chest. For formal occasions, he wears slacks instead of the shorts and tracksuit. Sagittarians have no dress sense whatsoever.

Women

Tweed suits, heavy-gauge surgical stockings, sensible shoes and waterproof backpacks are the order of the day for Sagittarian women when it comes to having fun. In the office, don't look for colour co-ordination. In fact, better not expect much co-ordination of any kind. Some Sagittarian women have been known to wear skirts *and* trousers on a cold day. As must surely be obvious, the Sagittarian female has little conception of making herself attractive to other people. She rates shin pads as sexy underwear, and indeed her best chance of making a favourable impression is probably going to come about by accident – not many lecherous Capricorn males are going to be able to resist the Sagittarian female jauntily jogging down the road to the hockey match in her old school gymslip!

MY FAVOURITE THINGS: SAGITTARIUS

Ronald Reagan, Charles Atlas, General Custer, Princess Margaret, Frank Bruno, *The Dukes of Hazzard*, Massey Ferguson tractors, Mark Phillips, Mickey Spillane, 007, Watney's Red Barrel, Idi Amin, Guy Fawkes, Gerry Ford, George Brown, medicine balls, Rachel Heyhoe-Flint, Attila the Hun, pyromaniacs, shopping trolleys, disaster movies, *Emmerdale Farm* reruns, Mary Decker, Ludwig of Bavaria, Coco the Clown, hoola-hoop trousers, *Midweek Sports Special*, David Coleman, Nigel Starmer-Smith, silage, The Wurzels, *The Times*, Ford Pintos, Matthew Kelly.

YOUR GUIDE TO LOVE: SAGITTARIUS

Sagittarius–Aries
Jupiter/Mars never was a happy conjunction and there is no way you can get along with a baby-like Arietan, who is going to be too weak to come on your fell-walking holiday and too cold to stand on the touchline for your big match. Best forget this one.

Sagittarius–Taurus
A Fire/Earth combo that could even work. Your Taurean lover is dull and conventional. Although you are clumsy and, on occasion, mindlessly violent, basically it wouldn't come as a major surprise to find you were members of the same golf club. You can do it, sports fans!

Sagittarius–Gemini
All kinds of planetary conflicts, not least the basic mismatch of Jupiter and Mercury, militate against this romance. You are simply not clever enough to combat this wily criminal's dishonest designs on you and your property.

Sagittarius–Cancer
Even if the stars could guarantee some kind of compatibility here – which they certainly can't – the briefest character analysis would rule this one right out. You like drinking from hip flasks, back-slapping, shoulder-pinching and hiking. Your prospective partner likes sitting in front of a micro eating crisps and tends to cry a lot. Leave well alone!

Sagittarius–Leo
You could be thinking that because you are both Fire signs, this Leo is going to desire you. Unfortunately, this is entirely erroneous and the important conjunction is that of the planets, Sun and Jupiter, which clearly spells disaster. The Sun outshines you a millionfold. The super-conceited Leo that you have your eye on probably doesn't even know who you are. Simply, a Leo wants love, life and hot cha-cha. Not really you, is it?

Sagittarius–Virgo
What are you, crazy? Virgoans go berserk if a speck of dust penetrates the air-lock front door. Can you imagine what would happen when you come home from a romp across the moors, treading mud all the way across the kitchen floor? Well try.

Sagittarius–Libra
You wouldn't put up with the Venusian dithering of one of these bimbos if you had to have them on your team for a rugby or hockey match, so why should you put up with it in a love-match?

Sagittarius–Scorpio
The presence of Pluto in the basically Mars-dominated Scorpio doesn't make a connection with Jupiter any more propitious. It's surely never a good idea to get involved with one of these cruelly sadistic characters, and in your case it's a particularly bad idea. You're too stupid to cope. You'll die!

Sagittarius–Sagittarius
Well! Truly a mindless combination – redolent not so much of the many planets but the even more plentiful vacuum between them. Let's face it – you could do an awful lot worse than blundering around the sports centre with a Sagittarian friend. If you can manage it without falling over, go for it.

Sagittarius–Capricorn
Unless you're rich, it's highly unlikely that you can be attractive to this creepy social-climber. And if you *are* rich, you won't be for long once the Capricorn's greedy pincers go to work. You're not smart enough for this romance.

Sagittarius–Aquarius
This ménage would link up Jupiter, Saturn and Uranus and if they all behave (which is a big 'if') there could be advantages for you both. For example, a wimpy Aquarian is never going to want the sports pages in the morning, and you're too thick to understand any other part of the paper except a certain page three.

Sagittarius–Pisces
Basically, you are rather a buffoon. Some people dislike you intensely, but most just laugh at you. It's not completely impossible that someone, somewhere, could learn to love you. So stop and think before you do anything really stupid – like getting involved with a Piscean. Nobody needs a Piscean, not even you.

SAGITTARIUS FOOD AND ENTERTAINING

Dining chez Sagittarius is going to be a bizarre experience. With typical energy and equal stupidity, your oafish host will spare nothing in an attempt to create an interesting meal. Crushing eggs in one hand, dropping them, shell and all, into a food processor which is in turn dragged on to the floor, the genial Sagittarian buffoon will regale you with stories of how long it took the pheasant to die in the Magimix, and how cheap the wine was in the supermarket.

First Course:
Game pâté (riddled with lead shot)

Main Course:
Puréed raw pheasant

Pudding:
Jam roly-poly pudding with dry bread rolls (for throwing)

SAGITTARIUS ON HOLIDAY

Life for most Sagittarian males is treated like a big Outward Bound course, so it follows that your rugged, Sagittarian pal is really going to major on the Great Outdoors for his two week break. This person just can't get enough of canoeing down dangerous rapids, or being pushed over the Niagara Falls in a beer barrel. Many Sagittarians volunteer to relax on a two week survival course in extremely bleak conditions. This is the person you meet on a dark night on Dartmoor. There is only a needle, thread, 6" Bowie knife and you between him and starvation. His eyebrows meet in the middle. It's minus 23 degrees and you're surprised to note he's wearing shorts. You never believed somebody's legs could be that hairy. Why is his backpack weighed down with 70 kilos of rocks? Because he's a Sagittarian male on holiday – that's why.

While not being as fitness-fixated as her male counterpart, nevertheless it has to be admitted that the Sagittarian woman on holiday is never going to be too far away from a tent, a large mallet for hammering in guy ropes, and the reassuring sound of tinkling billy-cans. The Sagittarian woman is a stickler for ozone and trapezing off the Old Man of Hoy. Her sturdy uncompromising legs have propelled her across some of the most inhospitable tracts of land in the world. She can shear a sheep in under two minutes, sink 16 pints with the best of 'em, trample on wild flowers, and make fire from rubbing tree trunks together. She's the type of strapping girl you want to have on your side if you're into tag team wrestling in mud, but is she the type of girl you want on holiday?

THE SAGITTARIUS EMPOYER

If you find you have a Sagittarian for a boss – well bad luck, unless you are a dog or a horse, in which case congratulations. These people are really so incompetent that the business is not likely to last long with one of them at the helm. If you are criminally inclined, however, it must be said that you have a good chance of becoming the person to put this fool out of business. Statistics show that most cases of fraud are perpetrated against Sagittarians.

THE SAGITTARIUS EMPLOYEE

If you have read this far and you still have a Sagittarian employee, chances are you are either a Sagittarian yourself or a spineless Pisces, Cancer or Libra. Sagittarians spell death to the efficient running of any business. They will destroy office equipment and company vehicles. They cannot understand the simplest order. They are forever trying to organize games of seven-a-side rugby during lunch. They should be fired.

YOUR SUN-CYCLE DIARY: SAGITTARIUS – NOVEMBER 23rd–DECEMBER 21st

November 25th
With Jupiter moving secretly across the third quadrant,

and you being a sporty type, it should not come as a complete surprise when you are asked by someone you have not seen for ages to turn out next week for rather a good local hockey team. You feel a bit chuffed and buy a new stick.

November 26th
You still feel chuffed. In fact, you are thinking so much about the Big Match that you drive through a red light and cause a multiple traffic accident in which your car is written off and an old people's home is reduced to rubble.

November 27th
Mars hovering on the edge of Venus. You are released on bail, and not due to appear in court until after the match. You clean your kit.

December 1st
The big day arrives. You miss the bus and feel pretty tired by the time you arrive on foot. You need not have worried. You are only the sub. After five minutes, however, the centre-forward gets a bad tackle and breaks a leg. You begin to strip off your tracksuit and limber up, but are alarmed to notice that rather than call you on, your team is rearranging itself by bringing the goalkeeper up to centre forward, and putting the centre-forward in goal, with the broken leg strapped to the post, which serves as a splint. At half-time your team is 13 goals down and finally you get the call: Go down to the pub to get the drinks in before closing time.

December 3rd
With Christmas as well as Uranus on the horizon, it now appears fantastically regrettable that you never

knew about the old tradition of substitutes buying drinks for both teams, all the officials and any supporters – in this case nearly a hundred – who care to come along to the pub.

December 8th
Your letter to the insurance company about the car accident is returned marked 'Not known at this address'. Mars is now lording it over everything in your Zodiac. Jupiter is nowhere to be found.

December 12th
Your bank manager has not heard about the substitutes and drinks rule either. This makes you feel rather superior.

December 15th
The bailiffs have not heard of it either.

December 17th
Help is at hand. You meet a man at the Salvation Army soup kitchen who has a sure-fire tip in the Derby. He persuades you to sell your watch and give him the money to put on the horse.

December 18th
Afraid that your friend may have been mugged on the way back from the betting shop, you contact the police. They point out that the Derby is run on the first Wednesday in June, and that the chances of your friend – who somehow never gave you his name – returning on that day with a bag full of money are slim.

December 20th
You write a note to Santa – asking for a new watch – and send it up the chimney. Your house catches fire, even though there is scarcely anything left in it to burn.

December 21st
In court. Prospects for the new year are not good. The magistrate's mother used to be a resident of the old people's home until you destroyed it.

YOUNG
CAPRICORN
MODEL
3° FLOOR

CAPRICORN

December 22nd–January 20th

'Even as night must follow day
So shall I rise and have my way'

Henry III, part I

An aura of quiet authority surrounds the Capricorn personality, a sense of aristocratic position and power. Controlled by the planet Saturn, Capricorn people are respectful of tradition and good at leading others. How carefully the devious, unscrupulous, lying little twisters born beneath the lecherous Sign of the Goat have tried to build this image! How assiduously they pretend to be what they are not, and how single-mindedly they set about obtaining what they should not be allowed to have!

Capricorn people are perhaps the most ambitious and manipulative in the whole Zodiac. They are social climbers to whom snobbishness is a virtue. They are ruthlessly selfish liars who will do anything to get ahead – and that does not rule out criminal acts up to and including genocide. Admittedly Jesus was a Capricorn, but astrologers generally agree that the Divine nature of His birth excludes Him from any of the usual calculations.

At an early age the Capricorn child learns to express a serene dissatisfaction with its parents, usually indicating that it wishes they were richer, more beautiful and more interesting. This early indication of snobbishness grows only stronger with age. When the child is old enough to steal a purse or pour sugar into a petrol engine, he or she will be a fully established little Capricorn with nothing but the purest contempt for any parental effort at a sensible upbringing – ready in fact to become the perfect Capricorn adult. Capricorns will use you, betray you, rob you and cheat you. When you feel your life is at a crisis and you're standing next to the cliff-edge, your Capricorn 'friend' is unlikely to be standing by you – more behind you actually. It's also well worth pointing out that Capricorns have gone down in history as easily the meanest Sign in the Constellation.

THE CAPRICORN MAN

These guys are dangerous and sometimes difficult to identify. At first you may not realize they are Capricorns because they will probably be lying about their birth dates, along with everything else. They will ingratiate themselves with flattery, but beware: the minute you have nothing more to give is the minute you become entirely disposable to them.

Capricorn men forge diplomas to hang on their office walls. They cheat at cards, and frequently wear hair pieces. If they think you are rich or famous or both they will undertake almost any act of humiliation to associate themselves with you. But if they find out you are less rich or less famous than they thought, they will exact a swift revenge – sometimes violent, always spiteful.

Some of them wear green Wellingtons and Barbour jackets and can be seen driving Range-Rovers round urban thoroughfares in an attempt to make it look like their purely city-bound existence is little more than a temporary frolic away from their massive estate. Country-bred Sagittarians, however, will note how these would-be huntin', shootin', fishin' types appear to be mortally scared of poodles and on closer examination are wearing their wellies the wrong way round. Capricorn men never pay for anything. They have been known to go into well-rehearsed fainting routines rather than pay for a round of drinks. Some of them even go so far as to sew up their pockets so that the act of physically handling over cash is rendered well nigh impossible.

THE CAPRICORN WOMAN

The Capricorn woman may come on like Mrs Miniver, but in fact she is just as greedy for wealth and social status as her male counterpart. If she thinks you can help her to what she considers to be her rightful place – namely the back seat of a Rolls-Royce, surrounded by Harrods bags – then she will offer the world. Please note, however, that at no time will she actually give it. Capricorn women lie about their age, their background, their feelings, their marital status and where they were last night.

Being seen is the big thing for Capricorn women. The ultimate achievement for them is to appear in the pages of *The Tatler*, but since the planets have conspired to make a large percentage of Capricorns into lifelong members of life's perpetual loser battalion, the pages of *Tupperware News* are going to have to suffice in most cases.

Like their male counterparts Capricorn women are

notoriously stingy, and it is their super cheap make-up – which they are unable to resist buying even when they have quite a lot of money – that makes them look so irretrievably cheap themselves. They make good 'personality girls' dispensing free cigarettes at snooker tournaments or trade fairs.

CAPRICORN SEX

Men

Capricorn men, like their female counterparts, are usually more interested in making a profit than in making love. The Polaroid pictures taken during that romantic evening are going to reappear, and when they do it's going to cost you money to get them back. The snob in a Capricorn man would far rather gaze in admiration at your family tree than at your exciting body, but the chiseller in him may well regard a night in a warm house with free breakfast in the morning, as the kind of incentive for which he will happily go through the motions of erotic delight.

Women married to Capricorns report that their husbands can be relied upon to act romantically only once a year – on their wedding anniversary. Then they come home from work and suggest going straight to bed 'just like the old days'. That wouldn't be too bad if it weren't for the fact that ten minutes later the Capricorn creep is fast asleep and snoring. It's all been a blatant excuse to avoid going out to dinner!

Women

Remember that Capricorns scarcely ever feel real affection for anyone and will probably be sleeping with you in order to gain money, prestige, promotion, an introduction to your best friend or a ticket to Glyndebourne. Their enthusiasm for physical relations with you will generally be in proportion to what you have to offer financially. It would be highly offensive to suggest that Capricorn women prostitute themselves for money, but it is a verifiable fact that they are light sleepers and it's boring to lie awake all night in a strange house. Why not have a look round, they think, and what better place to start the tour of inspection than their snoring lover's wallet?

All in all, if you're the kind of person who has something that a Capricorn female wants, chances are that you're the kind of person who can afford to ignore her. Do so.

THE CAPRICORN DRIVER

The Capricorn's car is usually sparkling, new and expensive. It is also either stolen or rented by the hour. This cunning inhabitant of the Tenth House is always trying to impress in a deceitful fashion. Note the pathetically vulgar slogan stuck in the back window of the hired Mercedes: 'My Other Car's a Porsche'. Pull the other one, wideboy.

Capricorns treat the roads as a metaphor for life: they simply have got to get ahead of everybody else, whatever the cost. Their viciously competitive style of driving is only bridled when they catch a glimpse of a Rolls-Royce or other car more expensive than their own. They then become cringingly deferential.

LET'S DRESS CAPRICORN

Men

Capricorns are deceitful people, so they like dressing up to look like something they are not. We have already noted the 'country gentleman' style affected by some Capricorns who, for reasons best known to themselves, believe that they can further their ambitions by looking like Mark Phillips. Others favour a plausible City suit. The more sober professions, which are after all the breeding-ground for most of the major criminals in the country, play host to quite a number of Capricorns. The ones who succeed best are those who remember to take off their mirror-shades indoors and renounce their favourite snakeskin boots for some more conventional footwear.

Capricorn men who have forgotten themselves and dropped their disguise can be seen in highly unpleasant suede blousons, white suits or fur coats. At heart, tacky.

Women

The Capricorn female is tripping out of the boutique with an armful of outfits. The owner of this establishment is doubly pleased: not only has she just made a lot of money, she has also shifted all the old stock left over from last year. Because the Capricorn woman has a very mean side, and it turns out that she is too stingy to buy her own magazines, so she ends up coveting the styles in the *Vogue* she reads in the hairdresser's, and that is twelve months out of date!

Being desperate social climbers, Capricorns like to imitate the stars of the moment, like Princess Diana or Victoria Principal. They force their frequently flabby bodies into designer jeans and couturier leotards. They wear fur coats to picnics and tiaras to barbecues. Nine times out of ten, however, they still get mistaken for hookers.

MY FAVOURITE THINGS: CAPRICORN

David Frost, *The Tatler*, Bruce Forsyth, Norman Fowler, *How to Make Friends and Influence People*, personalized briefcases, strobe lights, Britt Ekland, Royal Ascot, Paul McCartney, Jean Kirkpatrick, *Who's Who*, Dudley Moore, rented Mercedes, Nicholas Parsons, ID bracelets, Edward Kennedy, airline stickers on baggage, Des O'Connor, *The Complete Works of William Shakespeare*, drinks cabinet, *Debrett's Peerage*, knighthoods, Marti Caine, brandy alexandre, Patrick Lichfield, Koo Stark, fake fur, Steve Wright.

YOUR GUIDE TO LOVE: CAPRICORN

Capricorn–Aries
Look before you leap, goat feet! No way is this spoilt, bad-tempered juvenile going to dance to your outrageously selfish tune. Saturn can never stay in the same realm as Mars anyway. Leave well alone.

Capricorn–Taurus
This is more like it. Good vibrations in the Milky Way. Rampant insecurity and love of the conventional make

Taureans a great target for your wheedling schemes. Convince them that everyone holidays in St Moritz and runs joint bank accounts and your troubles will be over.

Capricorn–Gemini
There's barely a single star in the entire cosmos looking down on this love-match with anything but an expression of horror. No way can you get the better of this slimy schizo without an awful lot of effort, and even then it can't be worth it. So if you feel you're falling . . . just tell your Gemini to put the encyclopaedias back in the bag and get going!

Capricorn–Cancer
The chart looks very flat indeed. It's unlikely that a Cancerian is going to give you much trouble, but is a semi-detached full of anoraks and software the kind of future you had in mind? You can do better than this.

Capricorn–Leo
Plenty of favourable aspects here, with the Sun and Saturn combining nicely. The Leo craves flattery and attention and loves to be seen as generous and fashionable. You crave status and money. Work it out for yourself, horn head!

Capricorn–Virgo
Don't be fooled into thinking that an Earth/Earth relationship is going to be a natural winner. There are probably worse things than living with a Virgoan, but we haven't heard of them. This mean and humourless hygiene-obsessive is really going to make you work.

Capricorn–Libra
Libras could be the types to really like you. Or not, as the rather confused case may be. Can you cope with

this vacillating, moody and rather stupid person? Well if there's something in it for you, the answer is probably yes. You could do worse.

Capricorn–Scorpio
The constellations look crazy. Saturn meets Mars *and* Pluto. Earth encounters Water. You'll try anything to gain a crooked buck, but where's the percentage in being hung up by the toenails and beaten with a mallet? You love yourself. Scorpios hate people. It doesn't add up.

Capricorn–Sagittarius
In an ideal world, this is just the kind of clumsy buffoon, the kind of out-and-out loser that you could well do without. If you're really desperate – and you know a bit about being desperate – settle for this fool. But you won't be happy.

Capricorn–Capricorn
You should know enough about yourself to realize this double Saturn combination could never work. What a tragedy to discover on your honeymoon that you'd both been lying about that money! There's a whole world of Taureans out there, why ruin your life with someone as unpleasant as yourself?

Capricorn–Aquarius
In case you'd forgotten, you like money, fast cars, expensive restaurants and big houses, and you don't want to have to earn them the hard way. Aquarians, for your information, like whole food, macramé, obscure Polish movies and frisbees. Quite simply there is nothing here for you.

Capricorn–Pisces
Pisceans are so wet you could pour them into a bucket. Even someone as low down as you needs more of a challenge than this. Well, if you must, take the money, but leave the family heirlooms. You may need to come back for them another time.

CAPRICORN FOOD AND ENTERTAINING

These people don't much care what they eat as long as others realize it's expensive and fashionable. They love to buy ridiculously priced food from Fortnums and spend vast amounts on getting their pheasants helicoptered to them on the Glorious Twelfth. For this nouveau riche, the Beaujolais Nouveau can't arriver too soon.

Poor Capricorns aren't too fond of showing off their dismal habitats to visitors so an invitation to dinner is unlikely. As for rich Capricorns, they can't get enough of showing off their appalling homes and giving parties which may well feature a hired waiter. Don't expect the fare to be overgenerous though. Capricorns love to show off their wealth, but as to being generous hosts – well that's a completely different matter. This is what you might expect dining chez Mr or Mrs Wideperson . . . Yes, you've guessed it – empty plates and solid gold cutlery and you can't eat those, can you?

CAPRICORN ON HOLIDAY

Who said holidays had to be fun? Not a Capricorn. These people regard holidays purely as an extension of their working (scheming) life. They pay bills with 'bent' credit cards. They ingratiate themselves into the company of the rich and famous. They make a nuisance of themselves beside the pool and in the disco, where their mirror-shades are a ludicrous handicap. They prey on single people hoping for romance. They steal the towels from hotel bedrooms. They are no fun at all.

THE CAPRICORN EMPLOYER

This entirely unscrupulous hustler is not by any means a good person to work for, unless you have the kind of aristocratic background that will get you special favour from a social climber. As a boss, the Saturn-based Capricorn will tell any lie to make you work, break any law to avoid paying you and use any excuse to punish you severely. Get out while the going's bad – it can only get worse.

THE CAPRICORN EMPLOYEE

Remember the little creep who's always volunteering to clean your shoes and fetch your coffee? Well, watch out. Behind your back, this Capricorn is working out exactly what to do with the Polaroid pictures (they seemed so funny at the time!) of you and that Leo at last year's Christmas party. Capricorns have a saying: He who grovels in front of the desk, shall one day sit behind it.

YOUR SUN-CYCLE DIARY: CAPRICORN – DECEMBER 22nd–January 20th

December 22nd
A worrying day spent waiting for the post – some of the free gifts you saw advertised on a corn flakes packet haven't arrived and you need them in time to use them as Christmas presents.

December 24th
When no post arrives again this morning, it occurs to you that you could give the only present you have received so far – a pink hot-water-bottle cover from your mother – to your boss, thus enabling you to suck up and save money both at the same time!

December 25th–30th
Like last year, a quiet Christmas. But who needs friends? For the hundreth time, you go over *Debrett's*, counting all the famous people with your name. You don't know either of them.

December 31st
Like last year, a quiet New Year's Eve. You think of going to a party being thrown by David Frost and Patrick Lichfield, but even if you'd been invited, you probably couldn't have made it to New York.

January 2nd
Back to work and good news! With a peculiar smile, your boss thanks you for the present by inviting you to his birthday party at his country house. He's also a Capricorn!

January 5th
Final preparations for the big day. You stretch your credit card to the limit purchasing a new tweed ensemble, a full range of evening wear, a shotgun, a cricket bat, a cigarette holder and a travelling trunk.

January 6th
Slightly embarrassing. The house is extremely impressive, and you are photographed for *The Tatler* on arrival, but the guests are decidedly *infra dig*. Many of them appear to be cockneys with broken noses. They laugh at your clothes. Unable even to find your boss in the crowd, you leave early.

January 10th
It transpires that several thousand pounds have been stolen from the office. The police estimate it must have happened on the night of the 5th. With not a little smugness, you provide your alibi.

January 12th
When the police learn that you are a Capricorn, that your boss has a birth certificate to prove he's a Piscean and that he certainly doesn't own a stately home, they arrest you.

January 16th
Something to brighten your day in prison: your brief smuggles in a copy of *The Tatler*.

January 19th
Having finally admitted to yourself that there is no picture of you in *The Tatler*, you start to leaf through the only other reading matter permitted in the cell – *Police Review*. And there you are, pictured at a party of

ex-cons at a country house in Berkshire which has been converted into a rehabilitation centre! You don't understand it, but this must be your alibi! And then you notice the shotgun . . .

PEACE
LOVE
AQUARIUS
PEACE
ZAPPA
HENDRIX
LIVES

AQUARIUS

January 21st–February 19th

'Rocks have feelings too'

Petra Kelly

This is, as people born under this Sign will keep telling us, the dawning of the Age of Aquarius. Uncharitable types may remark that it seems to have been a long time dawning without getting much lighter, but let's face it, Aquarians have got to be optimistic. Born at the deadest time of the year with some of the dullest stellar influences in the entire Zodiac, they are bound to suffer from an inferiority complex and over-compensate accordingly. Rebellious, individual, intuitive and independent is how you might describe them – if you were being kind. But it's hard to be kind to someone as insufferably boring as an Aquarian. These (so-called) enlightened members of the Eleventh House are in truth some of the most blinkered and faddishly stupid people it's possible to meet. A sense of humour is entirely alien to Aquarians. They drone on about their moronic preoccupations for hours on end with never a glimmer of levity, never a moment of less than stupefying dullness.

It is the bizarre natal conjunction of Saturn and Uranus that makes Aquarians feel so different from everyone else, and so convinced that they have the answers to life's many questions. They are always looking for alternative lifestyles, basically because they are failures in conventional ones and need a new set of rules to live by – so much for the rebellion – and once they have become failures in the new way of life, they usually move on to yet another. Hippies are Aquarians, as are 90 per cent of the ill-complexioned weaklings and fatties that always seem to work in health-food shops. UFO fanatics are nearly always Aquarians, as are women who deliver their own babies, men who have friends who know someone who bends spoons, and children who prefer brown rice to ice-cream.

THE AQUARIUS MAN

The Aquarius male generally falls into two types, depending on the position of Saturn at his birth. With Saturn ascending, he will almost certainly be fairly tall, clumsy, bearded, bespectacled and very boring. Very likely a vegetarian of the proselytizing type, he will wear baggy cords and an old pullover that was last washed in a sheep dip in the days when it still had four legs. Not content to bore you to death with how you are killing yourself by drinking, smoking, eating meat and generally having a good time *sans* aduki-beans, this one is going to come right at you with the other barrel too. It could be the Greens (and we do not mean the prize cabbage he has grown on a mound of unmentionable domestic refuse), it could be CND; it could be yoga, it could be Jack Kerouac; at its very most terrifying extreme, as he sits there goggling at you from behind the wire rims, nervously tugging the wispy growth on his chin, it could be God. All you can do is grit your teeth and thank your lucky stars it is not life insurance. (The Aquarian likes to think of himself as far too idealistic and principled for *that* at any rate).

Saturn descending at birth can throw up a wide variety of physical types, but they all have two things in common: the ability to get carried away by something entirely trivial that they do not know anything about anyway, and a whimpering dependence on their mothers, which stunts all emotional growth. Again, this kind of Aquarius man gets a bit of a reputation for being a rebel, but it is hard to say why. Sure, he is different but who would want to be like him? Short answer: no one in their right mind, which is what the Aquarian generally is not. You have met them at parties: we are talking about the man in the brown nylon flares and the sandals, the man who has been reading about these really incredible experiments with ESP where a dog guessed how many people were on a bus in a city the other side of the world or very nearly guessed anyway, and did he tell you about an extraordinary experience of his and his Mum's when he was at the teacher training college? Brace yourself. These people are out on their own – by public demand.

THE AQUARIUS WOMAN

The Aquarius female develops along similar lines when Saturn is in the ascendant – in other words she will be a gawky, frumpy, self-righteous bore with a sense of humour you could fit into a thimble if she were not already using it for creating one of the interminable quilts or shawls that she is always making for people who are no doubt dreading having to receive them. Cuisine free of sugar, alcohol, salt and indeed flavour will be the order of the day here. The Aquarius menu of bean-burgers and lentil cutlets have led many a wicked Scorpio to remark that it's not just her conversation and her age that lead her to be described as a boring old fart. Like her male counterpart this Aquarian remains particularly parent-orientated. She is in love with her father and scared of her mother – an interesting state of affairs, since 90 per cent of abandoned children are eventually found to be Aquarians.

In some ways, the Aquarius woman born with Jupiter descendant is even worse, however. Her fads and affectations may not be as seriously dull as her sister's, but they certainly will not stand the kind of prolonged airing she likes to give them in the office: have you heard about the new all-in-one blender, mixer and dishwasher? Well you are going to. Have you heard about the new home computer (with second-generation nuclear melt-down capability available at small extra cost)? Stand by: did you know she has just started collecting Victorian lemonade bottles? What? You thought it was Edwardian lampshades? Oh no, that was never really a serious interest. Not like the lemonade bottles, and besides, that was last week. Grit your teeth again and once more thank your own stars it isn't life insurance. If it *is* life insurance, buy some and kill yourself.

AQUARIUS SEX

Men

Expect the unexpected is what they often say about Aquarians, and this applies to sex as much as to anything else. We won't go into why you find yourself having sex with one of these men – anyone can make mistakes – we will just concentrate on what might happen.

First, remember the Aquarian is prone to fads and fancies. It's your hard luck if he's on a celibacy kick. Even harder luck if he pulls out the old joss sticks and meditation manuals and suggests you try for 'the big one' – orgasm without physical contact. And it's strictly time to leave when the after-dinner conversation gets round to Scandinavian suicide-pacts. Put simply, there is no percentage in playing along with a loonie. This male, though, is more usually looking for a caring, dopey sort of mate. He may well decline to take off his wholemeal Jacob's wool double-weave vest in bed for fear of catching cold. He is not likely to be experimental or individualistic in his approach, despite the Aquarian character. The aspect of the fixed planets dictates that dullness be his overriding characteristic. Some virgins have gone to bed with Aquarians, a-tremble with expectation, but woken up the next morning not sure whether their status has changed or not, so paralysingly tedious has been their partner's performance during the night.

Women

It may not be this bad, of course. The health-food orientated Aquarius woman (Saturn rising) will be looking for a natural, no vitamins-added sexual experience. The man of her dreams need not bother polluting himself with after-shave, and his jockey-shorts had better be no less than 100 per cent cotton or he is going to bring her out in a rash. The Aquarius woman is really into consciousness-raising conversation, which rarely has the effect of raising anything else at critical moments. She believes that all natural body odours, hairs and smells are deeply erotic and she generally possesses more than most. Virgo males have been known to jump from very high windows rather than go to bed with these women.

THE AQUARIUS DRIVER

The average Aquarian drives a Citreon 2CV in rainbow paintwork with a *nuclear power, no thanks* sticker in the window. Some even more hard-line Aquarians only ride a bike, with a basket on the front and a baby in the back. A few more wealthy members of the set can afford to indulge their faddist nature. They could go for a De Lorean, a chicken-manure-powered Saracen armoured car or a four-wheel-drive diesel golf kart. Whatever you do, do not talk to these people at parties.

LET'S DRESS AQUARIUS

Men

Aquarians believe we are on the verge of a new era of enlightenment and wonder, yet most of them go about proclaiming the good news in clothes that make you wonder where you can get tickets to stay behind in the bad old days. Macrobiotic black smocks, ex-army greatcoats, patched loon-pants, open-toed sandals and collarless shirts are popular with these health-food fanatics. For the rest, the only rule seems to be: if it's wrong, it's right. Nylon shirts, dreary blue parkas, whacky yellow leg-warmers, clogs, cardigans, and floral ties. Aquarians get a reputation for eccentricity when they deserve one only for sheer stupidity. Do not be fooled into thinking that un-matched socks and un-zipped flies are somehow endearing. They are not.

Look more closely and you will find that this Aquarian's jacket being worn the wrong way round is not a rather charmingly absent-minded accident. The arms are tied up at the back. This man is mad.

Women

Again, you have to wonder how these people can claim to be looking towards a bright new dawn when they clearly brought their clothes in a very murky dusk. Calico wrap-around skirts, earth shoes, thick, spiky pullovers and Peruvian-style hats with matching gloves and socks are very much *de rigueur* for the Aquarius woman. Some exceptions go a more extroverted route and appear in hot pants, crocheted bikinis or woollen coats of rainbow design. Neither type could safely be taken anywhere.

MY FAVOURITE THINGS: AQUARIUS

Donovan, Friends of the Earth, Tea for the Tillerman, *Nuclear Power? No Thanks* stickers, herbal remedies, Sainsbury's Muesli, stripped pine floors, Edgar Broughton Band, Genesis, small is beautiful, Petra Kelly, World Wildlife Fund, the I Ching, Krishnamurti, Channel 4, David Puttnam, flared trousers, futons, non-alcoholic beer, National Film Theatre.

YOUR GUIDE TO LOVE: AQUARIUS

Aquarius–Aries

An Air/Fire combo which predictably leads to nothing but hot air. Having something of a complex about your parents, the last thing you want is to be in loco parentis yourself, forever changing the nappies of an Arietan partner. Give yourself a chance, and forget this one.

Aquarius–Taurus
Earthy Taureans are desperate to conform, and will certainly be embarrassed when you announce at a dinner party that your vegetarian principles not only forbid you to eat the boeuf bourgignon, but also mean you can no longer stay in the same room as this sumptuous repast. Your Taurean, being extremely greedy also, will not take long to decide which side to support.

Aquarius–Gemini
Mercury and Saturn collude to bring two Air signs together, but how long can it last? Life is one possibility – it's always a possibility for a Gemini, but with time off for good behaviour you may see your partner again in about fifteen years.

Aquarius–Cancer
The heavens have produced a nice little combination of constellations here and you could be in with a chance, provided your solar aspect can cope with the Crab's Pepsi-Cola influence. You can make muesli, your Cancer lover can play with a computer. You can be quiet together.

Aquarius–Leo
The stars look down, and can't believe it. You're not rich, good-looking, good fun or even particularly bright, so why should a Leo want you around? Well, the best that can be said for this relationship is that at least you won't upset your Leo partner's absurd sense of self-importance!

Aquarius–Virgo
Finicky hypochondriacal Virgoans! They may sympathize with some of your views on organic farming, but they won't want you tramping mud into the kitchen! And when was the last time you had a haircut? The last time you met a Virgoan, that's when.

Aquarius–Libra
Uranus crosses Venus, and you have some decisions to make – or rather, *all* the decisions to make. Can you cope? Maybe you can, dandruff and all, but is it really worth it?

Aquarius–Scorpio
You love fresh fruit, vegetables, peace and love. Frankly, when the poisonous Mars/Pluto influence brings down the fixed aspect of Paraquat on to all this, you're going to be a goner – but not before you've taken on board some peculiarly unpleasant experiences. If there is still time to escape, do so.

Aquarius–Sagittarius
A well known Air/Fire combination this. You are actually cleverer than someone else and you should push home your advantage. You're going to wind up with an entirely clumsy buffoon, of course, but being honest, how are you ever going to do any better?

Aquarius–Capricorn
There is plenty of Saturn in your make-up, but don't think that matches you to the Saturn-dominated Ram. At heart, you're a loser and a Capricorn is born to rip off people like you. The thing is, though, is there anything you have that the Ram will want?

Aquarius–Aquarius
The heavens seem to still their seasonal course. All is quiet. So go for it. Boring your Aquarian partner may be. Stupid, even, and not very attractive. But when was the last time you looked in a mirror, Aquarius? You two were made for one another.

Aquarius–Pisces
OK, you're a peace-loving type, but surely nobody loves *this* much peace! You won't have any arguments from your Pisces partner, but neither will you get much aggravation from your pot plant – and that's more pleasant to smoke!

AQUARIUS FOOD AND ENTERTAINING

By now you should have a fairly good impression of what to expect at an Aquarian dinner party. In a room painted navy blue with stars on the ceiling, a huge poster of The Jimi Hendrix Experience on the wall and a goat in the corner, expect no mercy from your very boring hosts.

First Course:
Wholemeal spaghetti with baked beans

Main Course:
Brown rice and lentil stew

Pudding:
Prunes

Cheese:
Goat-curd

Beverage:
Home-brewed real ale (non-alcoholic)

AQUARIUS ON HOLIDAY

Aquarians like to think of themselves as the least hide-bound and most adventurous members of the Zodiac, but in truth they are set in their ways. They don't like travelling abroad and they don't like going anywhere without being sure of a good supply of their favourite foods. Admittedly, many Aquarians claim to have hitch-hiked to Katmundu, but Aquarians are not the only ones who used to be hippies, and very often a little research will reveal that they are confusing their own real life experience working in a health-food shop in Brighton, with the exploits that actually happened to some Leo or Gemini friend.

THE AQUARIUS EMPLOYER

This sucker has got to be a good person to work for. You can always get round Aquarian bosses because, pathetically, they tend to see the best in people. Some employees invent complicated league tables for telling lies to the boss. The more outrageous your reason for not being at work, the more points you score – like 'I'm sorry I'm late – there was a bus strike in La Paz.' You work in Leeds!

THE AQUARIUS EMPLOYEE

This one is a gem, and if you have one, you are a lucky boss. Probably only the Piscean and the Libran are this malleable as employees. Not to put too fine a point on it, you can trample all over an Aquarian. Threaten to withhold her carrot juice, let down his bicycle tyres, confiscate their CND badges. Beat them if you are a Scorpio and this kind of behaviour appeals to you. You simply cannot lose.

YOUR SUN-CYCLE DIARY: AQUARIUS – JANUARY 21st–FEBRUARY 19th

January 21st
The Brazilian bean crop has failed. You abandon the kite you were making from a cheesecloth shirt and the frame of an old bicycle and rush down to the health-food store, where you buy up the entire stock of pulse foods.

January 22nd
A hard day's work reorganizing your house to accommodate the sacks of beans delivered in a truck by the happy health-store owner. Having filled the bedroom with lentils to a depth of three feet, you allow yourself a little smile – he obviously has not heard about Brazil yet.

January 23rd
Yesterday's newspaper, which you share on a co-operative system with some other Aquarians, arrives.

January 24th
You still cannot get over the shock of what you read in the paper. They grow only coffee beans in Brazil.

January 29th
The health-store owner still will not take back the beans and says he wants his money.

February 1st
Inspirational Virgo comes into the house of Capricorn ascendant and fired with the brilliance of a new idea, you set up a stall on the road outside your house with a sign saying: *Cheap Beans*. It rains.

February 3rd
A watery moon. Still raining.

February 5th
Still raining but you must persevere. While standing in the road, you notice there is a loose tile on your roof. You note that you must fix it sometime.

February 7th
The rain has stopped. Virgo now descends into Mercury. Things must be looking up. Feeling like a celebration bean stew, you run upstairs to the enormous store-cupboard that is your bedroom.

February 9th
You regain consciousness in a slimy heap at the bottom of the stairs. Slowly, you piece together what must have happened: the rain leaked through the roof into the bedroom, the lentils became soaked and expanded, you opened the door and were swept away by a green and red tide of wholefood.

February 10th
Bailiffs arrive with the health-store owner. You are forced to sell him your home at a ludicrously low price because it is in such a disgusting condition.

February 14th
Staying at your mother's, you still receive a Valentine card. Having no lover that you are aware of, you are tempted to think it must be for your Mum – but postmarked Honolulu?

February 16th
Cycling past the health-store, you notice it is locked up with a sign in the window which reads: *On Vacation*.

February 19th
With Uranus back-tracking across the galaxy and Mars in the ascendant, the portent for the rest of the year looks grim.

PISCES

PISCES

February 20th–March 20th

'In water, saw he only wetness'

John Milton

Easy-going, a fish drifting with the tide in the infinite depths of the sea – depths which only a solitary dreamer may truly understand. Generous to friends, but private and undemonstrative; the Pisces gift is to see more through the emerald facets of the ocean than the rest of us perceive through air. This is a deeply sensitive Sign, and the Piscean has a deeply sensitive personality.

Before we go any further, let us just correct this opening contradiction. *Pisces* and *Personality* are mutually exclusive terms. There is no such thing as a Pisces personality. Pisces people have no personality whatsoever. Look for the list of infamous Pisces people at the end of this chapter and you will look in vain. No Piscean has ever made it to any position of prominence in any walk of life. But if you think you know someone who *is* famous – or at least known to more people than mother, father and landlady – and who claims to be a Piscean, there are several easy explanations. Your acquaintance is really a Capricorn who is lying to you, probably out of sheer force of habit, or just as likely because he or she has a birthday so close to Christmas that there is a danger of only getting one present per annum. Alternatively this 'Piscean' could be a Sagittarian (too stupid to remember his/her proper birthday) or a Cancerian. Cancerians, interestingly – or more accurately uninterestingly, are very nearly as shallow and spineless as Pisces and many parents lie to them about their birthdays, sometimes merely for spiteful fun but often in order to move the date on to the Piscean 29th February, thus saving money on presents and parties for three out of every four years. The true Piscean is fundamentally weak, shy, short, utterly forgettable. There is one in every class or office or crowd – it is just that you do not always notice them. Dogs frequently mistake them for lamp posts.

Certain Mongolian tribes highly skilled with bow and arrow, allow Pisces children to grow up normally, and then use them for target practice. Barbaric perhaps, yet anyone who has ever met a Piscean will not be able to deny that there is a certain harsh logic in this practice.

THE PISCES MAN

If Walter Raleigh had had a Pisces male readily available, he would no doubt have used him instead of his cloak to lay in a puddle before Good Queen Bess. Pisces males are simply not worthy to be called men. They are unimaginably weak and pathetic. They will never ever stand up and fight for anything. On the beach, Pisces males have been known to die of suffocation, through having so much sand kicked in their faces by laughing Capricorns. At traffic lights, they often don't move even on green, for fear of offending the people waiting on red. They get mugged and apologize to their attackers. They calculate all expenses in multiples of Mojos, Fruit Salads and penny chews. They can rarely summon up the courage to ask for a drink, let alone a date, so unless picked up by strange women with even stranger tastes, they are likely never to have girlfriends. Sometimes, the only friends a Pisces male can find are other Pisceans. They talk about Neil Young and build balsa-wood models. If Darwin's theory holds any truth at all, the next century is going to see very few males born into the Twelfth House of the Zodiac.

THE PISCES WOMAN

Self-effacing is not a strong enough description for the Pisces female. Non-existent would be nearer the mark. These women are so insignificant, so totally lacking in personality of any kind that they are frequently classed as 'inanimate objects'. Some of them find employment as shop-window mannequins, although not many are good-looking enough. Some have been hired as spies – on the basis that no one could ever suspect them of anything – but since nobody ever finds them interesting enough to speak to in the first place, the custom has tended to be discontinued. Pisces women are sometimes picked up as a last resort by those males unable to do any better and have been known to protect their honour by boring their partner to sleep before he can make a move. Much given to knitting, these unremarkable creatures are as a blank sheet of paper that Nature forgot to write on.

PISCES SEX

Man

The Pisces man is like a fish in water – very wet. The Pisces man in bed is like a fish out of water – stone dead. Generally speaking, making it with a Pisces man is going to rate on your experiential score sheet somewhere between cutting your toenails and watching repeats of *Emmerdale Farm*. At least you are guaranteed a good night's sleep. The Pisces lover is, to say the least, ineffectual – he is so shy. You will be doing well if you can get him to take off his anorak. If you get past this, and you manage to persuade his mother, who will come to collect him at 10.30, that he has already left, you are in with a chance. But do not expect much in the way of technique – the Pisces man would not like to impose. And neither would he know how to.

Woman

Not many Pisces women have sex with men, for the simple reason that they are so staggering dull and unattractive that the men are rendered physically incapable. If you are a Scorpio or Capricorn you might prevail upon a Pisces woman to submit to your disgusting predilections and enjoy yourself that way, but otherwise you are in for a thin time of it. Pisces woman behave in bed as if they have learned about sex from a Mother Superior (and quite often they have).

THE PISCES DRIVER

You may well be asking, what car? Many Pisceans are incapable of passing their driving test, being simply unable to make the imaginative leap required to believe that you can sit down and travel along at the same time. Those that do get through, in their boring routine way, are the great motor companies' dream customer. These are people who do not get company cars but still want to buy a Vauxhall Chevette *anyway*. If they cannot afford a new one, they will go for a second-hand Escort or Austin Maxi. Pisces drivers always obey speed limits, brake going into every corner and stop at zebra crossings, even when there is no one there. They always honk if they know Jesus, but never if they had it last night.

LET'S DRESS PISCES

Men

All that is drab, dreary, boring, inconspicuous and unimaginative can be found hanging in the Piscean wardrobe. The summit of Piscean fashion is probably represented by a brown cardigan or a grey nylon anorak. Pisces men, being drawn to rain and cheap artificial fibres, love anoraks more than any other article of clothing. They never wear proper jeans or training shoes, but always the ASDA or TESCO equivalent. They hate the feel of cotton next to their skin. If, by mistake, they buy trousers that fit, they take them up by a couple of inches to reveal their white nylon socks. Pisces men think Millets is a super place with a great sense of style.

Women

Pisces women do not stand out in a crowd. In fact, they can be hard to locate in a couple. National Health glasses, Arran sweaters, hiking boots and bobble-hats are popular even in summer. Indian-print dresses and duffel coats are *de rigueur* for parties. Pisces women rate surgical knee-supports as sexy underwear. When it is raining, they can be seen on the streets actually *wearing* waterproofed tents and sleeping bags. For a Pisces woman 'the latest style' means only the wooden step through a hedge encountered on a recent rambling weekend.

MY FAVOURITE THINGS: PISCES

Little Weed, Starsky and Hutch, the Princes in the Tower, John Noakes, Kim Hughes, John Curry, Charlton Heston, rambling tours, motorway service stations, saying hello to policemen, milk chocolate, Anne of Cleves, Henry Kelly, collecting bottle tops, meals on wheels, lollipop men, Swiss Family Robinson, Jimmy Young, Scout and Girl Guide camps, *Diary of a Nobody*, *The Invisible Man*, Leonard Cohen.

YOUR GUIDE TO LOVE: PISCES

Pisces–Aries
A very doubtful stellar connection. The Aries personality is entirely childish and while you are spineless enough to fall in with their petty and changeable demands, it is almost certain that you are neither strong enough nor rich enough to cope with the task of looking after a person like this for 24 hours a day.

Pisces–Taurus
Improbable. This could be the most traumatic relationship you've ever been in. It is unlikely that your water-based Jupiter personality would be able to withstand the physical ordeal of being loved by an earthy, Venus-orientated Taurean, and you certainly could not provide the sort of continuous reassurance that this highly unstable personality will require.

Pisces–Gemini
You're the kind of person who finds enough trouble in life without having to go looking for it. This schizo-criminal is going to take you for everything you have. In no way can the universe be smiling on the meeting of your stars.

Pisces–Cancer
On the face of it, a good watery match and someone pathetic enough for you to live with – but beware. Cancerians have a nasty little reservoir of greedy deviousness which will find you, and roll you over in the end.

Pisces–Leo
This Fire/Water combination is a possibility. Leo people are very self-centred and don't like to be outshone, but there's hardly any likelihood of that happening with you around, is there? Leos love to party, and you will probably be put to bed before any fun starts. Just the way you like it.

Pisces–Virgo
Can you put up with being sterilized before breakfast? Yes, an astrological doormat like you can probably put up with just about anything. This could be a relationship made in heaven.

Pisces–Libra
The stars appear to be blinking on and off. Your Libra lover can't really decide about you. But that's all right really, isn't it?

Pisces–Scorpio
Ouch! Mars *and* Pluto cross your path. You'd better make a will before accepting a date with this one. What

would a twisted, vicious weirdo like your Scorpio friend want with a wimpo like you? It could only be your body. Probably in little pieces.

Pisces–Sagittarius
You're terrified of Sagittarians, with their alarming muscles. And as for the men . . .

Pisces–Capricorn
The constellations don't add up here, and this is a highly improbable romance, let's face it. Capricorns need people they can use and – except for some highly unethical doctors – no one has ever thought of a use for you.

Pisces–Aquarius
A romance not blessed with any discernible good influences. Aquarians are faddish people and will probably be looking for someone to share their interests. You are too boring to be enthusiastic about anything, really, but you may just squeak in if you step up your attendance at the macramé class.

Pisces–Pisces
Not a bad idea. This wet fish is unlikely to be attractive to anyone else and you're too dull to know why. You could sit around listening to Leonard Cohen and talking about horoscopes.

PISCES FOOD AND ENTERTAINING

Pisces people are very ordinary indeed. So is their food. They like everything bland and unexciting. They are scared of good restaurants, preferring to stick with what they know – Berni Inns and motorway service stations. Indeed, for a special occasion, like a wedding anniversary, it is not uncommon for a Pisces couple to travel more than a hundred miles along the M6 in their Austin Maxi in order to dine on plaice and chips at their favourite wayside Happy Eater. The Piscean ideal menu is:

Starter:
Prawn cocktail or soup

Main Course:
Steak and chips

Pudding
Ice-cream

Beverage:
Shandy

THE PISCES ON HOLIDAY

Pisces people really don't often get it together to go on holiday. They do however dream about walking tours of Wolverhampton and visits to the local library. Some cruel Scorpios take their partners winter-sporting in order to use them as toboggans, but usually the Pisces person is content to stay in the house with the television and a packet of salt 'n' vinegar crisps. Pisceans just wouldn't know how to have a good time, so it's best not to trouble them with one. Leave them at home.

THE PISCES EMPLOYER

This character is just a joke. Your only problem in working for a Pisces boss is the certain knowledge that the business will soon be going bust. Pisces people make dismal failures whenever they try to organize anything and their staff are certain to rob and cheat them at will. A Pisces born with Saturn rising into the Third House of Jupiter does, admittedly, have a little more chance of success but not much, owing to the correspondingly increased likelihood of having a chronic dandruff problem, which does little to attract new customers.

THE PISCES EMPLOYEE

In general, quite a good person to have around. A Piscean can be underpaid, forced to work long hours in an unhygienic environement, beaten and fired, all without a murmur of complaint. (Some of them do moan occasionally when stretched to the limit on the rack.)

YOUR SUN-CYCLE DIARY: PISCES – FEBRUARY 20th–MARCH 20th

February 20th
Saturn colludes with several malignant cosmic influences to get the week off to a disturbing start. On your way to work, you are tripped up by a toddler sticking its leg out of a push-chair. When you complain to the child's mother, she punches you in the face and demands your wallet. As ever, you decide that cowardice is the better part of valour.

February 21st
Feeling very low. Too embarrassed to report the loss of your wallet and cheque card, you have no money and not much food.

February 24th
The Dog Star rises in the House of Venus. You discover a spare tin of Pedigree Chum and devour it greedily.

February 27th
On the street, looking for scraps of food, you spy the woman who mugged you. Quickly you look the other way and make good your escape.

February 28th
Only 24 hours to hold out till pay day. The conjunction of Jupiter and Mars seems to promise a change of luck at last.

March 1st
With a degree of gloating amusement that is not wholly professional, the Accounts Department points out that this is not a Leap Year, there is no February 29th, and there is *no* pay. You suspect that everyone else got their money, but decide you had better not rock the boat by complaining.

March 4th
The office takes pity on you and hands you a 'wage packet'.

March 5th
The check-out girl at your local supermarket explains in a less than enchanted fashion that they do not take luncheon vouchers.

March 6th
You have a feeling that everyone is laughing at you, but decide it's probably best not to say anything.

March 14th
You finally pluck up the courage to tell the bank about losing your wallet. They are ridiculously kind about the whole thing and provide you with a new chequebook immediately.

March 15th
Spring is in the air. The axis of Pluto has turned towards the Vernal equinox. A bill arrives, showing that the credit card you lost with your wallet has been used to buy just a little more than £100,000 worth of goods up to and including March 2nd. You go to bed.

March 17th
Still crying, you go to the police. When at last they notice you, they laugh.

March 20th
Winter seems to return. Bailiffs remove the painting-by-numbers harbour scene your mother used to love so much.

FAMOUS PISCES PERSONALITIES

There are no Pisces personalities.

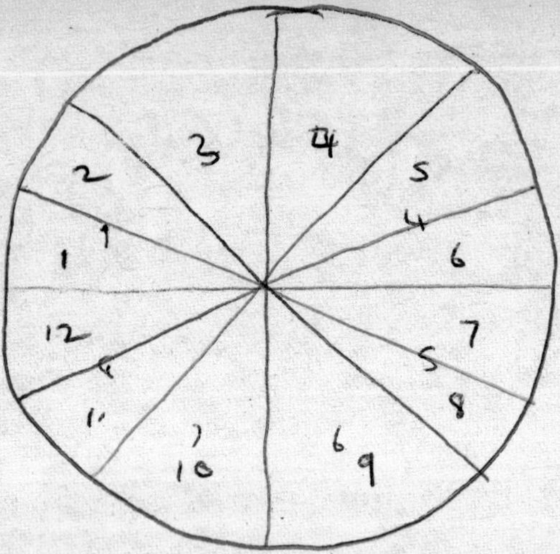

1
2
3
4
5
4
6
7
5
8
6
9
7
10
11
12
1

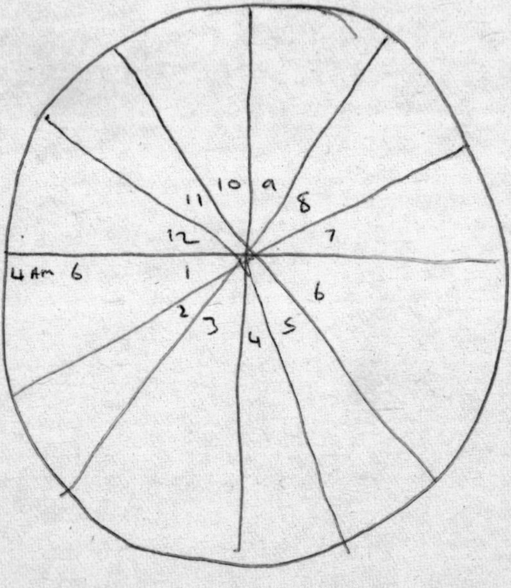

10
9
11
8
12
7
4 Am 6
1
6
2
3
4
5

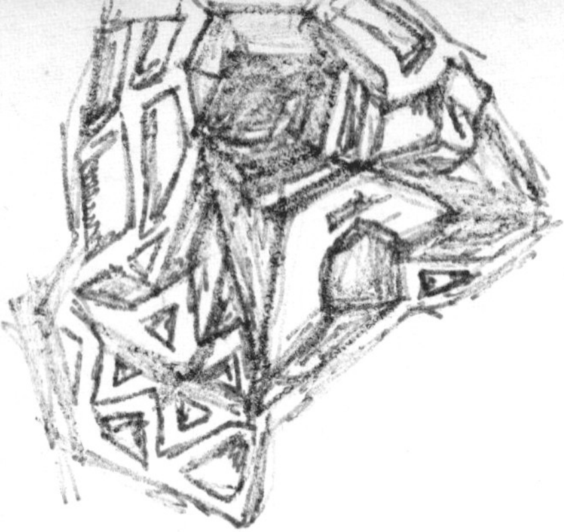